Trapped. . . .

Sondra raced down the hill, slipping, sliding through piles of leaves, running away from Curt and Mars.

Above her on the hillside, she could hear the men crashing through the undergrowth. Then she came to the electric fence, and there was only one direction she could run. The men in green were shouting to each other, and their shouting alerted the watchdogs, who began barking furiously. At least Jaeger and Mars would know that something bad was going down.

Then, ahead of her, a man slid down a gully and stopped, blocking her way. She didn't try to go around. She ran right for him. And when he put out his hands to grab her, she launched herself at him, ramming her head into his unprotected gut, driving him over on to his back. She fell to the ground on top of her victim, momentarily stunned, then rolled away, fighting to clear her head. She pushed up to her feet, took a shaky step or two, then fell again. By the time she recovered fully, it was too late. She was surrounded. . . .

THE NAZI HUNTER SERIES

Mark Mandell

NAZI HUNTER

Hell Nest

PINNACLE BOOKS NEW YORK

NAZI HUNTER: HELL NEST

Copyright © 1983 by Mark Mandell

An original Pinnacle Books edition, published for the first time anywhere.

First printing, May 1983

ISBN: 0-523-41599-0

Cover photograph posed by a professional model.

Printed in the United States of America

PINNACLE BOOKS, INC.
1430 Broadway
New York, New York 10018

HELL NEST

Prologue

August 26, 1947

Goga Tepes shoved the plate of tortellini aside, a scowl contorting his broad, lumpy face. As far as the Rumanian was concerned, a loss of appetite was akin to impotence. Both involved human weakness. Both were unthinkable. And yet this evening, try as he might, Tepes could not put a single forkful of food in his mouth.

Despite the oppressive heat and humidity of the windowless monastery cell, his fellow diners were having no trouble downing the meal. Well into their fourth bottle of *vino bianco,* the five Germans joked and laughed while they gorged themselves on tidbits of meat-filled pasta.

Tepes watched them feed. Beneath a heavy brow ridge, his dark, hard eyes glittered. Compared to him, his tablemates were small, insignificant men. And the war crimes that they were bragging to each other about, the deeds that had earned them the right to travel the ODESSA secret pipeline to Argentina and freedom, were likewise small and insignificant.

Of the five, only one claimed to have

3

killed face-to-face. The ruddy-cheeked man sitting directly across from Tepes was a former SS-*Scharführer* (Staff Sergeant) who had overseen the premature burial of a few dozen Jews in Latvia. The other Germans had served in the SS too, but as bureaucrats of Hitler's "Final Solution." Their crimes had been committed with strokes of the pen, with forms filed in triplicate, crimes against victims they never saw. It was only natural that men of such feeble malevolence would look up to the Scharführer with admiration and awe. They sat beaming while, for the third time since breakfast, he related the story of the late-summer planting of the Latvian field.

Tepes shifted position on the hard bench, then leaned back against the stone wall, his massive arms folded across his chest. As he watched, the ruddy-cheeked man quickly warmed to his audience, shouting orders to imaginary storm troopers, gesturing violently at invisible Jews. The tale he was retelling with such exhuberance was one of blunder and stupidity. Because the mass grave hadn't been dug deeply enough, some of his would-be victims had managed to claw their way back to the surface of the field.

The story's all-too-familiar denouement wrought peals of laughter from the bureaucrats. Amid the uproar, the Scharführer caught Tepes glaring at him. The German's lopsided grin faltered, then faded. Tepes continued to glare. It was the Ger-

4

man who finally broke eye contact, his ruddy cheeks turning beet red, his grin returning, broader than ever, but wooden, sickly.

"*Bitte schön*," he said as he reached across the table for Tepe's empty glass and the straw-wrapped wine jug. Hands that had wielded a spade against defenseless human heads trembled slightly as they sloshed cool fluid into the tumbler. When he replaced the glass in front of Tepes it was dappled with greasy fingerprints.

"*Einen Trinkspruch!*" the Scharführer said, lurching to his feet, hoisting his glass high in the air. "*Vogelfrei!*"

The others jumped up at once, raised their glasses and shouted, "Vogelfrei!"

Tepes did not move, either to stand or to touch his glass.

Thinking that the Rumanian didn't understand the meaning of the toast, one of the bureaucrats set down his wine and did a little pantomime. He made flapping movements with his arms. The others found this hysterically funny.

Tepes grimaced at their backslapping and forced laughter. The gallows hung over them all. He could smell their fear, and worse, he could smell his own; he could taste it in the back of his throat. The pantomime was unnecessary. Tepes had heard the toast before. It meant literally "free as a bird." In the case of the assembled war criminals it translated more precisely into "free until caught." Either way,

5

the toast no longer strictly applied to Tepes, who had been caught but for the moment was still free.

After more than two years on the run, after internment and processing through four different Displaced Persons camps, when he was finally moving along the SS escape route, he had been recognized. It was not as ironic as it sounded, given the nature of that route and the state of world politics at the time.

SS war criminals fleeing prosecution traveled an established path known as the *Vatinkanische Hilfslinie,* or "monastery route." It was made up of a chain of friendly Jesuit and Franciscan monasteries. The chain began in Hamburg, Germany and ended in Belgrano, Argentina. Along the way, stops were made in Austria, at Innsbruck and Kufstein, and in Italy, at Bolzano and Genoa. Tepes was in Bolzano, roughly 200 miles from Genoa and boat passage to South America.

The trouble with the monastery route was that the Catholic authorites were catholic in their acceptance of refugees. They didn't discriminate between Rumanian Jews and Rumanian Nazis, as both were escaping the communist oppression that had swept over their country. Though the church did its best to keep potential adversaries apart, mistakes did happen.

Earlier that afternoon, as Tepes strolled alone in the cloister's inner courtyard, he had been confronted by one of his Jewish

6

countrymen. The balding little man had demanded money in return for silence. Right away Tepes sensed something was wrong. The Jew was more than overly calm; he was cocksure. And he already had the meeting place and time for the blackmail payment picked out. It had all the earmarks of a trap. A trap set by the "Jewish Brigade," a group of skilled Haganah assassins scouring Europe, sworn to avenge the six million dead.

What fraction of that number was actually on his hands even Tepes did not know. He had served as a volunteer in *Einsatzgruppe* "D," an SS mobile killing unit of battalion strength working in Rumania and the neighboring Southern Ukraine. The Einsatzgruppen were one of Adolf Eichmann's budget-cutting measures. They spared the expense of transporting victims to the death camps by murdering them close to where they were found. Victims were selected, brought together, held in restraint, transported to the place of death, counted, stripped of possessions, shot and buried. Careful records were kept, personal goods shipped back to the Reich. In two years, Tepes' unit, some 500 men, had murdered a quarter of a million people. Because the killing was done by firing squad, because there was so much of it, it was very difficult to keep track of an individual score. Simple long division gave Tepes 500 kills between 1941 and 1942. Long division, of course, didn't take into account his penchant for the work or his ability to command animals like himself.

As the leader of a squad made up of fellow Rumanian fascists, members of the notorious "Iron Guard," he had distinguished himself in the eyes of the SS. He had been awarded the "Cross of Merit" for the "psychological discomfort" he and his men had inflicted on the enemies of the Reich. The medal had meant nothing to Tepes; to the Haganah it was the badge of an arch-fiend.

Tepes looked at the Germans standing around the table from one sallow face to the next. There was only one capital crime among the ranks of the fugitive SS, and he had committed it. He had been discovered. To admit that he had been caught to these men, to ask them for help, was to ask for a bullet through the eyes while he slept or a dose of cyanide in his breakfast tea. Rather than risk their own precious safety by fighting the avengers, they would murder him and leave his corpse in some public place. And to make sure no one missed the point, they would carve a swastika into his forehead.

"*Kommen Sie, trinken*," the Scharführer said, waving for him to get up and join them.

Tepes pushed away from the wall, reached out and wrapped a huge hand around his glass. When he rose from the bench the others reflexively shrank back. He towered over them. Raising his glass in the

air, he said in German, "To our Brotherhood."

"*Die Kameradenwerk!*" the Germans
chorused, clinking their glasses together.

Before they could drink, while their arms
were still outstretched, Tepes squeezed
down on his glass. It shattered with a high-
pitched crack. Glass shards and wine
sprayed the table, the food, the Germans.
Tepes opened his hand. It was not cut but
it was wet from the wine. He wiped it on
his shirtfront.

His companions were slack-jawed, speech-
less. If he could have killed them at that
moment without penalty, he would have
done so. To cleanse ODESSA of such sniv-
elers he would have drawn the Sauer Model
.38 automatic pistol from his pants pocket
and, one after the other, blown their brains
out. But he could not kill them tonight
and count on moving to the escape route's
next "safe house" tomorrow. Moving on
was all that mattered to him. Unlike his
companions, Tepes had a mission in life, a
secret mission given to him personally by
Hora Sima, the national leader of the Iron
Guard. Tepes was to seek out a safe haven,
a place where he could build a new "nest"
of followers, where the power of the Iron
Guard could be reborn.

With a snort of contempt he put a hand
to the heavy table and pushed it aside.
There was nothing but silence behind him
as he walked to the cell's ancient wooden
door, opened it and stepped out into the

arched stone hallway beyond. He walked straight to the communal bedroom the SS fugitives shared. He'd had all afternoon to make his plans, to gather up the things he needed to implement them. Under his mattress he'd hidden an extra loaded clip for his pistol, a three-foot coil of piano wire, a pair of heavy work gloves, and a dark brown Franciscan monk's habit.

He removed the gun from his pocket and put it on the bed before attempting to pull on the habit. Though it was the largest one he had been able to find, the fit was terrible. He got it on over his chest only after exhaling and holding his breath. When he inhaled, there was a loud ripping sound as the back and armpit seams gave way. The hem of the garment barely covered his shins; the sleeves ended just past his elbows. None of that mattered, however. Those he passed in the moonless night would not be able to make out such details. And when it came time to hide, the habit would blend well into the shadows. He twisted his upper torso from side to side, further splitting the robe, giving himself a bit more space to breathe. The extra clip, the gloves and the wire he packed into the habit's front inside pocket. He carried the pistol in his hand as he left the bedroom.

By the time he slipped out of the monastery's side gate, he was drenched in perspiration. Normally, the town of Bolzano, high in the Italian Dolomites, cooled off after sundown. Not so this day. It was as hot at 10 P.M. as it had been at noon. And the air was deadly still. Tepes moved to the unlighted side of the street and started walking briskly east.

The cobblestone avenues were deserted, but lights were still on in many of the houses. As each house was blocked off from the street by a high masonry wall, Tepes could only see into the second-story windows. Through the open shutters, he saw people just beginning their suppers. They had put off the meal, hoping for some relief from the heat, but had finally given up, realizing that it wasn't going to get any better. Those in the darkened houses, those who'd already eaten, were on their beds, sweating, praying for a hint of a breeze.

Tepes took a right turn and the scenery changed abruptly. It had been modified by the advance and retreat of three different armies. The houses were bombed-out wrecks, the street pocked with shell craters, and operational lamp posts were few and far between. His destination, the cemetery of Santa Sophia, lay in the middle of the devastated area.

He followed the main avenue to the mouth of a street that, after a dogleg to the right, dead-ended at the cemetery's entry gates, where the payoff was to take place. Because of the dogleg, Tepes could not see the gates from where he stood. Conversely, no one at the gates could see him. To the left, a row of buildings was in ruins, its bricks, timbers and plaster strewn out into the middle of the street. To the right, the sidewalk was bordered by a high wall that enclosed the cemetery grounds. Just before the street made its dogleg turn there was a lighted lamp post. Near the streetlight the wall was breached by a bomb blast. If it wasn't already occupied by his opposition, it was a spot made to order for Tepes.

He didn't head down the street, but walked past it, along the cemetery's wall, until he found another large break. After thumbing down the Sauer's cocking lever, he carefully climbed over the breach and into the graveyard.

The place had taken a real pounding from shell fire and bombs. Everywhere there were shattered tombs, craters, mounds of heaved-up earth. Even in daylight it would have made a treacherous obstacle course; at night it was just short of suicidal. Tepes' only consolation was that his pursuers had to deal with it too. He moved at a snail's pace, picking his way around the piles of rubble, stopping often to listen.

He was roughly two-thirds of the way to the gates when his caution paid off. A hard metallic sound made him freeze in his tracks. It was the sound of a submachine gun bolt being charged. It came from up ahead, in the pitch blackness. Then he heard a whisper. It was answered by a voice to the right, a hushed, urgent voice.

Tepes didn't understand the language, but he recognized it at once. It was Yiddish. He kneeled down, his pulse pounding hard in his temples, the pistol grip suddenly slippery in his hand. He had been right. It was a Haganah trap. They had set up an ambush, a crossfire inside the cemetery gates.

Tepes knew that if he'd had five Iron Guardists with him, he could have turned the tables on the Jews there in the darkness, taking them out one by one. Alone, he stood no chance whatsoever.

He retreated to a position behind the breach in the wall near the streetlight. The avengers had stationed no lookout there, choosing instead to concentrate all their firepower at the gate. He crouched in deep shadow, tucking his pistol inside the habit's rope belt, pulling on the thick gloves and uncoiling the strand of piano wire. He knew he was in a tight spot. He had to intercept the Jew who'd recognized him before the man entered the cemetery. If Tepes was to move on with any hope of safety, he had to kill the man right under the nose of the Haganah.

And his plan had one serious drawback. If the Jew chose to walk on the other side of the street, keeping away from the streetlight, the piano wire would be useless. To use the pistol would alert the avengers. Yet Tepes had already decided that no matter what the cost, the Jew who had betrayed him would die.

13

The sound of a shoe crunching down on a bit of mortar sent a shiver up Tepes's backbone. If it was the Jew, he was early. But not early enough. Tepes raised himself up slightly, craning his neck so he could see over the top of the breach. The footsteps were very close. And they were on his side of the street. Then a short, balding man in his early fifties stepped into the glow of the lamp post. It was the Jew.

For a split second Tepes paused, letting his quarry move past the break in the wall, then he jumped over it, swinging in right on the man's heels. The Jew heard the noise behind him, but it was too late. Tepes had already made a loop of the wire by crossing his wrists. He was already dropping the loop down over the smaller man's head, past the point of his chin. Before the Jew could turn or cry out, Tepes jerked the wire tight with all his strength, lifting up at the same time.

The Jew was hauled off his feet, tempered steel wire slicing into his flesh like a razor. Blood, black in the hard light of the street lamp, splashed over Tepes' gloves. The Jew went rigid, then wild, kicking at his attacker, clawing at the wire cutting deep into his neck.

Tepes abruptly turned him and with a shoulder drove him face-first into the wall. The kicking stopped for a few seconds, long enough for Tepes to twist the free ends of the wire together, locking the garotte at the base of his victim's skull.

When the kicking resumed, it was less enthusiastic and less coordinated. The man's strength was slipping away. Tepes turned him back around into the light, holding his shoulders pinned against the wall. The Jew's face was swollen and dark, his nose bleeding profusely, his tongue protruding from between bared teeth. The frantic clawing of the man's fingers at the wire gradually slowed, then stopped, and his hands dropped down from his throat and hung limply at his sides.

Tepes stared into the bulging eyes, watching as the pupils dilated, expanding outward until they almost completely covered the irises. The Jew was dead. Tepes had no way of telling whether or not the man had been conscious during those final seconds. If he had been, then his last sight on earth would have been the face of his murderer. It was a thought that pleased Tepes very much.

He let the corpse slip to the ground, then grabbed it by the ankles and dragged it over to the breach in the wall. He tumbled the body over into the shadows, removed his gory gloves and tossed them in after it.

As Tepes walked away, he considered the long, uncomfortable wait in store for the avengers. They wouldn't discover their dead kinsman until dawn. By that time, Tepes would be well on his way to Genoa.

Chapter One

Curt Jaeger parked the rented Firebird in front of the Piedmont address and shut off the car's engine and headlights. The black-haired girl in the passenger seat looked out her window and up at the two-story, vintage 1930, white stucco house. Like the other residences in the Oakland hills suburb, it was perched on a steep slope, high above the street, and commanded an excellent view of the twinkling lights of the city and Bay Bridge.

As Jaeger reached for the door handle, his pretty passenger turned toward him. "This is really dumb," she said.

Curt stared at Sondra Ben Solomon. Her sweater and jeans were black; her dark hair fell almost down to her waist. Amid all that black her pale face seemed luminous.

"Your FBI man could have a dozen armed agents waiting for us up there," she went on. "It could be a trap."

"It could be, but it isn't," he said. "McFee wouldn't go back on his word."

"His word? This guy is a career Bureau

man, a twenty-year veteran. Do you really think he's going to risk anything for the likes of us? Do you think it matters to him what kind of promises he makes to a couple of fugitive terrorists?"

The big, sandy-haired man frowned. In the week he'd been recuperating in the girl's company, they'd gone over this same ground many times. "We're not in jail thanks to him," he said, flatly.

"But my brother is," she countered. "Maybe this McFee has changed his mind about letting us run loose, too. He could have, you know. Curt, we don't need him. We're sticking our necks out for nothing."

"I figure I owe him this visit. If you want, you can wait out here. If I'm not back in five minutes to tell you everything's okay, take off."

"You're not serious?"

He tossed her the keys to the Firebird.

"No way!" she said, taking his right hand and slapping the keys back into his palm. She opened her door, got out, then slammed the door shut.

Curt was careful not to smile. If there was one thing he'd learned about Sondra Ben Solomon, it was that she couldn't stand being left out of anything, even a potential trap. He got out of the car and together they started climbing up the three tiers of cement stairs to the house's broad front porch. The shades on the ground floor were all pulled down, but when he knocked on the door he could see into the place through the door's beveled glass window. There was a great deal of dark wood paneling, dark, heavy ceiling beams and built-in bookshelves tightly packed with a jumble of hardcover and softcover editions.

"Come in," said a gruff male voice.

Jaeger opened the door and entered. Sondra brought up the rear.

Their host was sitting in a red leather armchair near the unlit fireplace. He was dressed in a pale blue flannel robe and matching pajamas. His left shoulder bulged enormously under the garments. It was heavily bandaged and his left arm was in a sling. He was alone.

"I'd get up, but you know how it is," Special Agent-in-Charge McFee said.

"Yeah, I know," Jaeger said. McFee didn't look good at all. His face was almost as gray as his bristling crewcut. Bullet wounds did that.

"Sit down, please," McFee said, gesturing at the sofa across from him. "I'm glad you decided to come. Both of you. You saved my life down in that BART tunnel and I wanted the chance to thank you again in person."

"We exchanged favors," Curt said. "You let us go when you could have busted us. We're even."

Sondra didn't think so. "What about my brother Rick?" she demanded. "He's no more guilty of terrorism than we are, but he's still in jail."

"That was out of my hands from the

21

beginning," McFee told her. "If he'd been with the three of us, out of sight of the other agents in the operation I'd have let him go too. He wasn't. From what I understand, he'd be out on the street now if he could make bail."

"Yeah, half a million dollars' worth," she said.

"What can I say? The government takes a dim view of people who try to carry automatic weapons onto public conveyances. I'm sure he'll survive until his trial."

"Whatever," Sondra said, folding her arms in front of her chest. "It's no skin off your's now, is it?"

"Lady, you don't seem to appreciate the risk I took in letting you two go." The SAC indicated Jaeger with a nod of his head. "Your buddy, there, made the 'Ten Most Wanted' list this week. I've logged a lot of hard years with the Bureau. If I get caught in this, they're all down the john."

"She appreciates it," Curt said.

Sondra glared at him.

"Since I put my career on the line for you two," McFee said, "I think I deserve to hear the whole story."

"What do you mean?" Jaeger said.

"I've read the official police accounts of what you're supposed to have done, both here and in Europe over the last few months. I've also read your Special Forces service record. For me, the two don't jibe. Unless you've flipped out. And you don't

22

strike me as a nutcase. I want to hear your side of current events."

"It's a long story and it doesn't make sense unless I start at the beginning."

"I've got all night."

Curt stared down at his hands for a moment, gathering his thoughts. When he spoke, he looked up, straight into McFee's eyes. "My father is a Nazi war criminal. His name is Horst von Jäger. He was an SS military engineer during the war. He developed and perfected the gas chamber. He made mass murder practical. I didn't learn this until a couple of months ago, after my foster mother passed away. She and my foster father kept me protected from the truth for as long as they lived. They told me I was an orphan. They thought the past could be buried, forgotten. It can't. I found out that in 1949 the Allies captured a man they believed was my father. They tried him and imprisoned him in Germany. I went there, to face him, but the man in jail wasn't my father. He was an imposter. He told me that my father is free, alive and prospering thanks to the international criminal syndicate he has behind him. It's known by many names: ODESSA, the Brotherhood, *Kameradenwerk*. It's made up of the former leaders of the Nazi movement, ex-SS men and their offspring. You've heard of it?"

"Yes," McFee said. "Go on."

"The man in prison told me something else," Curt said. "He told me that my father had my mother put to death in his machine when she became a political embarrassment to him. My father's crimes weren't impersonal any more. I knew how the relatives of his victims felt. I was one of them. I swore I'd get him, I'd kill him myself. I resigned my commission in the Army, smuggled the imposter out of prison and ran straight into a group of my father's men. Thanks to my military experience and bloodline, I was a prime candidate for recruitment by ODESSA. They even had a special job all picked out for me to handle. I let them believe I was joining them. Then I made them pay. The place was called Schloss Grausheim, the Austrian castle where my father carried on his experiments, the place where my mother was murdered. I leveled it. And when Grausheim's commandant got off on war crimes charges for a second time, charges I arranged to be brought against him, I executed him myself on the steps of the courthouse."

"What about the ski resort in Bavaria?" McFee said. "You were involved with the Mossad in that deal, right?"

"I was involved," Curt said. "My father was the engineer on the ski resort project, too. It was his last assignment for the Fatherland. A ski resort for bigwig Nazis. Only the ski resort was just a front. Under it, in a cavern in the mountain, was a secret repository for SS gold. I knew that the Israelis were going to try and take the

place to get the gold back. And I also knew
that the man who was running the ski
resort operation was the same man who
worked with my father during its construc-
tion. So I volunteered my services to the
Mossad. I'd go in and scout it out for them
in order to get a crack at grilling the boss
man on the whereabouts of my father. I
found out that he was in Los Angeles."

"Which brings us to the assault on the
Interglobal Oil skyscraper in downtown
L.A.," MacFee said. "What was its connec-
tion to your father and this Kameradenwerk?"

"It's still connected," Jaeger corrected
him. "It's a major cog in the Brotherhood's
worldwide economic empire. You see, what
these guys did was ship their war booty to
South America far in advance of the armi-
stice. By the time the war ended, they had
hundreds of millions of dollars safely
tucked away in Peruvian banks. They used
the money to make a financial base, in-
vesting it, taking over key companies. For
thirty-five years they've been expanding,
ensnaring the world in their economic web.
Now they believe it's come time to take
political control, to establish the 'Thousand-
Year Reich' Hitler promised. The trouble
with these ex-SS men is that they're still
the same as they were way back when.
They run their corporations the same way
they ran Germany; with intrigues, back-
stabbing, infighting. That was the reason
my father was sent to Los Angeles from

Paraguay. To settle the power struggle going on for control of Interglobal Oil. He settled it by putting out a contract on the then-chairman of the board. I hit Interglobal but missed my father by a half-hour."

"Hit?" McFee said. "You mean you blew the top off the building and left corpses sprawled all over L.A."

"They killed a good friend of mine," Jaeger said. "Someone who had no part in any of this. Someone I dragged into the deal. I owed them for that. I still owe them."

"Which brings us to the terrorist attack on the Bay Area Rapid Transit system," McFee said.

"That's right," Curt said. "While I was at Interglobal Oil I got my hands on a document that contained part of the Kameradenwerk's plans to bring down the U.S. government. The idea was to start a campaign of terrorism so vicious that the American people would cry out for repressive laws, stronger leaders—in essence a peaceful takeover by ODESSA's agents. It was to begin with a rush-hour attack on the BART system by a group of escaped convicts. When I couldn't get the legitimate authorities to listen to me, I got the help of Sondra here and the Zionist Defense Group. We had everything prepared to take out the convicts, but you FBI guys stepped in and messed things up."

McFee smiled. "We had information leading us to believe that you were the ones about to highjack the subway train."

"You mean you had an informer?" Sondra said. "Someone in the ZDG?"

"Not a very good informer, I'm afraid," McFee said. He looked at his shoulder. "His mistake nearly cost me my life."

"You look like hell," Curt told him. "Should you be out of the hospital so soon?"

"No, I shouldn't," McFee admitted. "But I couldn't very well ask you to meet me there. And I wanted to hear your story."

"You believe me, then?"

"Yes, I believe you. But I'll tell you flat out that I can't bring any of what you've told me to the Bureau's attention."

"And why not?" Sondra said.

"Not enough solid proof that this isn't just some paranoid fantasy."

"But you just said you believe me."

"I do. That doesn't mean my superiors will. Look, these multinational corporations are tough enough to nail even with great evidence. It gets to be a political thing real fast. You mess with them, close them down, and you put people out of work. That doesn't go over big in an election year. It's going to take some time to set this thing up right, to make it foolproof. If I jump right into it with both feet, the deal will get blown and no one will ever take it seriously again."

"And what are we supposed to do for a couple of years while you're getting your case together?" Sondra said.

McFee didn't answer.

"Curt, I told you this guy was a jive artist," she said. "He isn't going to help us. He's snowing us."

Curt stared at the SAC. "She's got a point," he said.

McFee grimaced and shifted in his chair. "I can't get you off the hook with the Bureau. It's too late for that now. But if you insist, I can give you a gesture of my good faith in all this."

"What kind of gesture?" Curt said.

"I think I can put you back on the trail of your father. That's what you want, isn't it?"

The tendons in Jaeger's square jaw flexed. "Yeah, that's what I want."

"A few years back I handled a CIA confidential request for additional information on a fellow who lives in upstate Michigan," McFee said. "Enclosed with the request was the CIA's sanitized file on the man. He calls himself a priest. He's not. He's an expatriate Rumanian, an organizer in the local Rumanian community, an anticommunist hero. According to the file, he organized anticommunist resistance both here and in his native land, under the guidance and financial support of the CIA. It was the CIA that sponsored his admittance into this country and for a while he was under their heaviest protection. Now he can take care of himself. The quasi-monastery he runs could double as a fortress. And it is staffed by a paramilitary force. According to the file, when he was in Rumania during the war he was part of the Iron Guard."

"The what?" Curt asked.

"It was the political arm of a religious group, the Legion of the Archangel Michael. They used a combination of mysto-Christian dogma and fascism to draw the peasantry into their ranks. The Iron Guard wore green shirts instead of brown but the mentality was exactly the same. During the war, this guy enlisted in the SS and worked in one of the Einsatzgruppen. I take it you know what they were?"

"I know."

"Our priest recently imported a couple of his old running buddies from Rumania by way of Paraguay. He has lots of contacts there. He exports 'work crews' made up of local yokels he's trained. All of them from solid Rumanian peasant stock."

"Work crews?" Jaeger said.

"Yeah, that's what it says on the documents. The training he gives them is paramilitary. The same old shit he was doing before 1940."

"What's this guy's name?"

"Tepes. Goga Tepes."

"Can I see this file on him?"

"I don't have access to it anymore. I think I can help you another way, though. An old friend of mine, ex-Bureau, took an early retirement up in that area. He and Mr. Hoover didn't see eye-to-eye on the proper width of a gentleman's necktie. His name's

Zebulon Mars. Call him Zeb. He's been up there hunting, fishing, drinking for the last ten years. He does some guiding during the season. He's a good man to have at your back. I can phone him and tell him you're coming."

"That would be fine."

"If anybody in this country knows where your father is, I'd bet on Tepes," McFee said. "I just wish I could be there when you wring the information out of the bastard."

"I wish you could be there, too," Jaeger said. He got up and extended his hand to McFee. "Thanks for everything," he said.

Curt and Sondra let themselves out. She said nothing until they were back in the car. When she did speak, what she had to say was entirely predictable.

"His 'good faith' gesture was pretty slim, if you ask me," she told him. "I'd call it tossing us a scrap."

It was predictable, and it was true.

"Maybe," Curt said, "but it's the only starting point we've got, other than Paraguay. I don't intend on dropping in down there without a solid idea of what the opposition has in store. If I can pick this Rumanian's brains about the ODESSA setup in Paraguay, I can plan an attack." He started up the car. "The real trouble right now is that we don't know enough about Tepes or his pals. We don't even know what they look like."

As he pulled the Firebird away from the curb, Sondra asked, "Where to?"

"Telephone," he said, heading for downtown Oakland. "It's time to call Italy."

In the parking lot of an all-night doughnut shop, Jaeger found an empty phone booth. After feeding the machine five bucks in assorted change, he was connected to the number he'd dialed. It rang a couple of times, then someone answered.

"*Pronto?*" said a cranky, old man's voice.

"Jonas?" Jaeger said. "This is Curt, calling from the States. I've got to talk to Geller."

"Geller's gone. He was called back to Tel Aviv yesterday. The Mossad board of inquiry is going over his case."

Jaeger frowned. The case in question was the fiasco at the Bavarian ski resort. Wolf Geller had been the Israeli Secret Service commander who'd headed the operation. Now his head was on the chopping block. The Mossad did not like grandstanders; it liked negative publicity even less. And it had gotten plenty of that, what with all the civilian casualties involved. Given the nature of the disgrace, if Geller hadn't been a major hero there wouldn't have been any board of inquiry; he would have been out on his butt.

"I'm in kind of a fix over here," Jaeger said.

"So what else is new?" Jonas answered. "I've been watching the reports out of San Francisco. They're blaming the BART at-

31

tack on those ex-convicts. No mention of ODESSA. No mention of you, either."

"I have it on good authority that I'm on the FBI's most wanted list."

"Congratulations."

"I also think I may have a lead on the whereabouts of Horst von Jäger. It involves a man the CIA repatriated, a former Rumanian Nazi now living in Michigan. His name is Tepes. Goga Tepes."

There was a silence at the other end of the line. Then Jonas said, "Say again."

"A Rumanian. Goga Tepes. You've heard of him?"

"I've heard of him."

"This Tepes and a few of his friends from the good old days are running a school for neo-Nazis. He's exporting teams of paramilitary-trained men to South America for reasons that aren't clear as yet. It definitely has something to do with the Brotherhood operation in Paraguay. The bottom line is I need some help in identifying Tepes and pals. I could use photos of him and his known associates during the war. I could also use any dossiers you might have on this guy. Anything that would give me an insight into his character, tendencies and the like. He's got a small army of men to protect him and he's locked himself up in a fortified position. I need an angle to work on him. Will you send me what you've got?"

"No," Jonas said.

"No?!"

"I won't send them. I'll bring them."

"This is not your kind of shindig, Arnstein," Curt said. "There's going to be a firefight for sure. People are going to die."

"Better at least the right people should die. I'm coming. Where should I meet you?"

From experience Jaeger knew that it was a waste of time to argue with the old man. "It'll take three days to get there by car. Can't risk public transportation. I can pick you up in front of the Detroit International Airport on the fifteenth at noon. Can you make that?"

"Easily. It'll only take me a day to get things settled here. I can fly from Milano the day after tomorrow. See you at the airport."

The phone went dead.

Curt hung up his end and walked back to the car.

"Well?" Sondra said through her open window.

"Let's get some doughnuts and coffee to go," he said, jerking a thumb back at the enormous, flooodlit stucco doughnut that graced the shop's roof. "It's going to be a long night."

Chapter Two

Goga Tepes glanced up from his opened text and stole a peek at the CIA man who was sitting in a back pew of the small chapel. Hat on his lap, the government agent was watching the proceedings with feigned disinterest. Tepes fought back the urge to grin. He and the CIA had been partners of sorts for almost a quarter of a century. He had seen agents come and go, some to an early grave, some to retirement, but none of them had failed to be moved by the sacrament of the Iron Guard. Because none of them were Rumanians, none really understood the meaning of the ceremony. Understanding, of course, was not a requirement of an emotional response.

The men of the Iron Guard were forged together by three things: an intense hatred for everything not Rumanian, not Orthodox Catholic, for everything intellectual, communistic, Jewish; a love for their native soil and its noble peasantry; and the bond of their living blood.

The chapel's cherrywood altar was ringed by tall, ramrod-straight blond men. All were in their early twenties, all were wearing dark green shirts of military style with leather Sam Brown belts. Each of the them had his right sleeve rolled up over his bicep. They were farmboys no more. In their steely gaze there was resolve, determination, power.

Tepes turned away from the podium to the short, rotund man to his left. The man was Ante Palac, an old comrade from the Einsatzgruppe days. Palac's hair had long since vanished but his eyes were still hard, brilliant blue. Ante Palac held up to him the golden chalice and a tourniquet. Tepes took the tourniquet and advanced to the closest young man.

The brawny fellow did not object when Tepes took hold of his bared arm and lifted it out, away from his body. He stared dead ahead as Tepes knotted the length of latex tubing tightly above his elbow. Tepes turned to the right. Waiting for him like a faithful old dog was his other friend from the old days, Vlad Curoscu. Curoscu hadn't aged so well. He was scrawny, his eyeballs yellowish, his face blotched with liver spots, and his green shirt seemed large. Curoscu held the white enamel tray. On the pad of cotton on the tray were twenty-three disposable hypodermic syringes. Tepes took a syringe, deftly inserted it into the young man's bulging vein, and withdrew ten c.c.'s of his blood.

Ante Palac stepped forward, holding up the golden chalice. Tepes spoke a few words of Rumanian, then squirted the dark red fluid into the cup. He discarded the syringe, took a fresh one, removed the tourniquet from the first young man and applied it to the second. He took the same amount of blood from each man in turn, finishing up by repeating the process on his helpers and himself. He held the chalice by its graceful stem, swirling its contents round and round, mixing, mingling them.

Then he faced the altar and the gilded plaster icon of the Archangel Michael, and raised the cup of blood to it. He spoke a prayer aloud, and when it was said he brought the gleaming cup to his lips and sipped. He held the precious liquid in his mouth for a moment before swallowing, savoring the sharp metallic tang. From the corner of his mouth a drop escaped, a single bead of ruby red ran down his chin. He passed the chalice to Vlad Curoscu who swirled, prayed, sipped and passed it on.

The cup of blood moved down the line. None refused to drink. None gagged.

Tepes again looked at the government agent. Was the man's face slightly green? Tepes warmed to the thought. The CIA went to great lengths to train its men, to ready them for the unknown, yet they were soft, weak. Compared to his legionaires, they were cringing little girls. It was Tepes's philosophy of training that made the critical difference. He trained not only the body but the mind. He took his men into the belly of the beast, showed them what they were capable of, the brutalities, the butcheries, then taught them to turn it on and off like a faucet.

The blood-drinking sacrament showed more about the mettle of his trainees than a bucket of medals, a hundred make-believe battles. It showed their total commitment to the Guard, to him. It showed the extent of their personal power over themselves, over normal human desires. It was the combination of commitment and power that made them men to be feared, men to be trusted with even the most disagreeable of tasks. Men who in the cause of the Kameradenwerk were absolutely invaluable.

With a few words of Rumanian, Tepes dismissed the troops. He walked down the center aisle, his long black robe swishing the ground. the CIA man rose as he approached.

"I hope our little ritual didn't upset you, Mr. Welch," Tepes said.

"Different strokes," Welch said. His mouth was a tight, hard line. "Is there somewhere you and I can go for a private talk?"

"Of course. Follow me," Tepes said. He led the CIA man through the back doors of the chapel to a small but sumptuously furnished office.

After Welch had taken a seat on one of the purple velvet chairs, he said, "May I be perfectly frank with you?"

Tepes stared at the agent for a moment.

He didn't approve of Welch's hairstyle. It was over the tops of his ears. He didn't approve of the roundness of the man's belly under the vest of his three-piece gray suit. Welch was badly out of shape. Furthermore, Tepes didn't approve of Welch's opening line. Frankness had never been part of the Rumanian's relationship with the CIA.

"By all means," he said, taking a chair behind his leather-topped desk.

"The company is very concerned about you," Welch told him.

"About my safety? Surely that cannot be in question."

"No," Welch said. "Your safety is not in doubt. Even if someone broke your cover now, it would take so long to get you deported that the law suit would outlive you. What the company is worried about is your little program here. You seem to have stepped up the intensity considerably of late. You're training with automatic weapons and heavy assault gear. The company would like to know exactly what it is all for."

Tepes smiled. As the skin of his face tightened, the lumps in his cheeks and chin stood out in high relief. "You never seemed concerned over my training program before," he countered easily. "I've been working with the local youngsters here for almost twenty years. If you've studied my dossier, you know that in 1955 I supplied the company with a squad of highly skilled, Rumanian-speaking guerrillas who were subsequently dropped behind the Iron Curtain."

"To perform acts of sabotage and organize anticommunist resistance," Welch said. "That project turned out to be a complete disaster. None of your men was ever heard from again."

"That was not my fault. If there was a security leak, it was at your end. Surely my credentials as an anticommunist are not in question here."

"Let me put it another way, Mr. Tepes," Welch said, looking down at his lap, fingering his hat brim. When he looked up, he looked straight into Tepes's eyes. "In order to get the company to help you enter this country, you made a lot of big promises. You claimed to have a cadre of dedicated men still in Rumania who would follow your orders. You claimed to have access, through members of this cadre, to top-secret military information. You said you could provide us with details of troop movements, defenses, dossiers on top party officials. None of that, I repeat, none of that has ever materialized. To date, the company has spent a great deal of money and manpower to give you and your friends what amounts to complete amnesty for war crimes you committed while members of the Waffen—SS."

"It's a little late for your people to back out of the program, isn't it?" Tepes said. "If you pull the plug on me and it gets out that you protected a mass murderer of my caliber from prosecution, how will it look?"

"We do not want to pull the plug," Welch said. "We do want to know why you have assembled this group of men, where they are going, and for what purpose."

"Let me assure you it has nothing to do with Rumania," Tepes told him. "I would never attempt any kind of 'Bay of Pigs' type action. And certainly not with only twenty men."

"Where, if not Rumania?"

"I'm afraid I cannot be specific without breaking my oath of secrecy on the matter."

"Be general, then."

"South America."

"For what purpose?"

"To aid the government of a staunchly anti-communist pro-Western country. One of the United States's best allies in the region."

Welch fingered his hat brim some more. "You mean Paraguay, don't you?"

"I didn't say that."

"But for the last twenty years you have been sending men there. One or two at a time. According to their travel documents they were all supposed to work on cattle ranches. Are the twenty men here now going to work on cattle ranches, too?"

Tepes smiled again. Then he looked at his watch. "Ah, Mr. Welch, you're going to have to excuse me for a few minutes. Everything here is run on a strict routine.

We have a drill scheduled for eleven and I just have enough time to get into position to oversee it. If you like, you can watch. Or if you're tired from your trip, I'll have you shown to your room. We can continue our discussion later."

"I'll watch," Welch said.

"Very well." Tepes removed his black robes and hung them on a brass and walnut tree. Under the robes he was dressed as his men had been: in forest green shirt and slacks. He also had the same chest-crossing leather belt and harness. At his hip, looped through the belt, was a holster. Under its snap flap was a Smith and Wesson revolver. It was a stainless steel model with an 8⅜-inch barrel chambered for .44 Magnum. A real hogleg. On the other side of his belt, in a slim leather scabbard, was an SS killing dirk with death's head pommel.

"We can get the best view of the operation from the tower," Tepes said. "This way, please." He walked past the CIA man and out of the office, down a long corridor that opened onto the refectory dining hall. On the other side of the dining area he opened a door that, in turn, opened into a steep flight of wooden stairs.

Tepes started up, listening to the sounds Welch made as he tried to keep up. Puffing, panting sounds. The government agent was indeed out of shape. The tower room was nothing more than a small turret-like structure on the roof of the main building. Surrounded by unshuttered windows, it was full of bright summer sunlight. It was barely big enough for two men.

Welch's face was flushed as he stepped up beside the much taller Rumanian. "Hell of a view," he said, wiping his nose with his handkerchief.

Tepes nodded. From the tower, one could see almost the entire grounds of the estate, a 360-degree panorama. To the north was a broad patch of dense timber, pine and birch. The woodlot ended about 500 yards from the main building and was replaced by neat, cleared fields, their stone fences covered with summer grasses. Between the timber and the fields was a dirt road. To the west was the remains of an old iron ore mine, its decaying crane and conveyors just visible over the tops of the trees. To the east and south, on the low rolling hills, was the town of Harberstam. Sunlight glinted off the white church steeple. Everything was lush and very green. Beyond the fields and woodlot, encircling the whole estate, was a twenty-foot-high electrified fence. Inside the wire was a separate fenced dog run inhabited by Dobermans and Alsatians.

"What sort of drill is this?" Welch said, squinting under the shade of his hand.

"It's what I like to call a 'live drill,'" Tepes said. "I've divided my men into two groups. Five to protect, six to attack. There, you see?" He pointed at a cream-colored

Mercedes convertible full of men in green shirts that had appeared on the dirt road at the extreme left of their field of vision. It was traveling at a high speed, bouncing over the ruts, throwing up a cloud of pale brown dust behind. "That is the protect team."

"And where is the . . . ?"

Welch broke his question off. The answer was right out there in front of him. Another car, this one American-made, a heavy, powerful sedan, roared out of the shade of the woodlot and jolted to a sudden stop in the middle of the dirt road. The plan was to block the road. It didn't take into account the suicidal derring-do of the Mercedes' driver, who floored his accelerator and bore down on the sedan at full speed.

The occupants of the sedan opened fire on the oncoming convertible. The muzzles of automatic weapons, Heckler and Koch G3s, stuck out of the car's windows. After every few pops of blank round there was the solid, hornet whine of a real bullet.

"Jesus!" Welch said. "Those guys are using live ammunition!"

"One round in ten is live," Tepes said, without taking his eyes from the enfolding drama. "It adds considerably to the spice, don't you agree?"

The Mercedes cut over hard left at the last instant, swerving around behind the sedan, then back onto the dirt track on the other side of it. All of the convertible's

occupants were well down below windshield level. It was just as well, as the
windshield was pocked with a number of
bullet holes.

The driver of the sedan threw his machine into reverse, backing around to pur-
sue the escaping convertible. Before he
could get going in forward, the driver of
the Mercedes slowed his car to a stop about
fifty yards away. One of his passengers
stood up in the back seat. In his hands he
had a short, olive-green tube affair. He set
the tube on his shoulder and looked down
the sights.

"Oh, my God," Welch said. "That's a
LAW!"

The men in the sedan saw it, too. They
bailed out of both sides of the car, hitting
the dirt and rolling away. Rolling away
just as the LAW went swoosh, jetting
smoke and flame from its tailpipe, while
from its mouth shot a high-explosive projectile. It ran in a track straight as a
draftman's line, right into the engine compartment of the sedan. The car exploded,
doors, hood and trunk lid flying, and then
burst into flames.

The driver of the Mercedes didn't stick
around to watch the show. As soon as the
projectile was off, he threw his car into
gear and sped away. He only got about
another twenty yards before there was a
sudden flash under his right front wheel—a
flash, then smoke, then the hollow whump
of an explosion. The car rolled onward on

three wheels. Then two more explosions took out both the back tires. Crippled, the Mercedes bounced to a stop.

Small arms fire crackled back and forth between the two opposing forces for a moment, then Tepes reached for a button on the window ledge. It activated a siren. At the sound of the horn, all hostilities stopped.

"So, who won?" Welch said.

"It wasn't that kind of drill," Tepes assured him. "It was an object lesson for both teams. A very important lesson. The men in the Mercedes should not have run. They should have pressed their immediate advantage after the explosion and finished off their attackers. Then they should have returned the same way they came, via a route they knew was safe. If those Claymoore mines had been fully armed, the protectors and anyone they were protecting would all be dead."

"And the guys in the sedan should have rammed the Mercedes instead of trying to block the road," Welch said.

"Correct. They did show some quick thinking when they saw the LAW, however."

"You could have lost half your squad if they hadn't abandoned ship like that," Welch said. "I'll say one thing for you, you sure do take some hairy chances."

"I try to make the training as realistic as possible. Believe me, it pays off. Now, I really must see to my men. There is a debriefing to be done before we take lunch."

"We haven't finished our talk," Welch said.

The Rumanian was already climbing down the steep stairs, forcing his guest to hurry to catch up.

Ante Palac was waiting for them at the doorway.

"Show Mr. Welch to his quarters," Tepes told the plump little man. "After lunch we can talk some more about your company's worries."

Tepes smiled and left before the CIA man could protest. He headed for the debriefing room, which was across the monastery's compound yard. The sun was hot on his back as he crossed the open area. The dogs in their wire pens barked and jumped as he passed. He was not displeased with the performance of his men. The mistakes they'd made were to be expected, given their experience in organizing their own manuevers. And in Paraguay, they would not be asked to do any planning of their own. The men Tepes had already sent, men with years of experience in protecting the elite of the Kameradenwerk, would be the ones who would lead. What was required of the trainees was that they be utterly fearless in the face of hostile fire. They had proved themselves that.

This squad was more than a feather in Tepes's cap. It was the crowning glory of his life. What triumph that the inner circle of pure blooded Germans, the men who ran the Brotherhood's international criminal syndicate, came to him, a Rumanian, for their palace guards. And palace guards was exactly what they were. A team of hard, ruthless young supermen dedicated to the cause of the white race and the ultimate redemption of their lost mother country.

It had not been an easy road for Tepes. It had taken years of performance on the part of his pupils to coax the inner circle away from their home-grown Teutonic bodyguards. Consistent performance was what counted, what achieved results. And now the Kameradenwerk high command had requested an entire platoon of legionnaires, not only to guard their personal safety but to perform acts of intimidation and murder within the borders of their adopted country. The heads of the Brotherhood had come to trust Tepes implicitly. Not just for his training program, either. He had the uncanny knack of being able to pick out men with the same talent he had, a talent for killing.

cle of pure-blooded Germans... Harper who ran the Rockefeller's international trade unial syndicate, using as front a Rumanian

Chapter Three

_____

As Jaeger drove the Firebird past the United Airlines passenger loading zone, an elderly man standing by the curb waved at him. He was short, bald except for tufts of snow white hair above his protruding ears, and deeply suntanned. He wore a striped T-shirt and baggy gray corduroy trousers. In his right hand he held a briefcase; at his feet were two small suitcases.

"That's Jonas Arnstein, the guy who brought all those Nazis to trial in the fifties?" Sondra asked as Curt swerved the car over to the curb.

"Yep."

"He's always been one of my heroes. But God, he's so little. He's a pixie."

"Not to ODESSA," Curt said, shutting off the engine. He got out of the car and walked around to where the old man stood. Jonas didn't even look at Curt. He was staring at Sondra. Curt could tell he was upset. His leathery face was all screwed up, as if he were wincing from some sharp inner pain. Jaeger extended his hand. Jonas shook it perfunctorily.

53

"So, how was your trip?" Curt said.

"I've had worse. Who is the girl? You didn't mention her on the phone. What is her part in this?"

Jaeger knew the old man well enough to anticipate his concern. "She's okay, Jonas. Believe me, she knows how to take care of herself. She's a member of the Zionist Defense Group."

"An urban terrorist?" Arnstein said, taking a step to the side so he could see around Jaeger's broad chest.

"Urban activist," Curt corrected him.

Jonas clucked his tongue. "What's her specialty? The pipe bomb?"

"I've got a great idea," Curt said. "Why don't you get into the car and ask her yourself? We've got a six-hour drive ahead of us and there'll be plenty of time for you two to get acquainted." He put the suitcases into the car's trunk, then opened the passenger door.

"Sondra Ben Solomon, this is Jonas Arnstein," Curt said. "Your childhood hero."

Sondra smiled fetchingly. "This is a real pleasure, Mr. Arnstein. And it's true what Curt said. I've admired you and your work for a long time."

"Such a beautiful girl to be a pipe bomber," Arnstein lamented to Curt.

"Get in the car, Jonas."

"I'll sit in the back, if it's all right," the old man said.

Sondra pulled her seat forward and

Jonas slipped into the back seat with his briefcase. As Curt pulled away from the curb, he said, "What's the latest news on Wolf Geller?"

Jonas leaned forward, putting his hands on the front seats' head rests. "There is no news. But the signs are all bad, I'm afraid. It looks like he will be dismissed from the Secret Service."

"For him that would be kinder than a desk job until retirement. A desk job would kill Geller."

"I've known Wolf for almost thirty years," Arnstein said. "He is my dear friend. He has his faults. He tends to overlook obstacles, to go off half-cocked, to forget that everyone isn't like him. In certain instances, like Ice Giant, those faults can bring harm to innocent people."

"Then you think he ought to be kicked out of the Mossad?"

"Whatever I think doesn't matter. The Mossad will act in its own best interests." Jonas turned to Sondra and said, "So, why is a lovely girl like you mixed up with a group of *goniffs* like the ZDG?"

His sudden question took Sondra aback for a moment. Before she could answer, Curt butted in. "Lay off, Jonas," he said.

"No, that's all right," Sondra assured him. "It's a legitimate question. The ZDG has gotten a lot of bad publicity over the years. Most of it was the result of FBI meddling. They infiltrated the organization in the early 1970s, worked their way up into the leadership, then agitated for violent acts. When the sheep followed, they were all busted. I joined the ZDG because my brother, Rick, was involved with them. This was long after the string of pipe bombings and arrests. My brother did a lot to change the group's image, at least locally. Nowdays we're more a community service organization. We run neighborhood security patrols, deliver hot food to the bedridden, things like that."

"Also, I think you do a little gang war on the side," Jonas said.

"I don't have to tell you about how the persecution started over in Europe," she said. "Nazi gangs roamed the streets at will, beating people up, vandalizing stores and homes. We don't have any intention of letting things go that far a second time. When people are threatened on the street, when homes are defaced, we fight back. We break some heads."

"And if that isn't enough?"

"We counter with exactly the same force that was applied to us. It's the same code the people of Israel use."

"The code of Hammurabi."

"An Israeli?"

"No, a king of ancient Babylon."

"I take it you brought the files on Tepes?" Curt said, interrupting the conversation before Arnstein could begin a lecture on moral philosophy.

"Yes," Jonas said, turning back and opening his briefcase. "I have them here." He took an old photo from the bulging folder and handed it to Curt.

Jaeger held it in his right hand and drove with his left. The picture was a black and white candid shot of a group of SS men in battle uniform. They were sprawled on the ground in front of a stone wall, mugging for the camera, pretending to be pouring what had to be "liberated" champagne over each other's heads.

"He's the big ugly one in the center," Arnstein said.

"You aren't kidding," Curt said. "He must be six foot five or six."

"Six seven and three hundred pounds when that was taken sometime in early 1941," Jonas said. "He was twenty years old at the time. And already a squad leader in the Einsatzgruppen. Those men with him are his squad. Most of them were part of his Iron Guard unit formed before the war."

"Twenty is damn young to head a squad," Curt said.

"A born leader," Jonas said.

Curt handed the photo to Sondra. She studied it for a minute, then said, "Our friend in the FBI told us something about the Iron Guard, but what exactly did this Tepes do? I mean, in the Einsatzgruppen?"

"Among other things he participated in the massacre at Kiev in the Ukraine in which more than 30,000 Jewish men, women and children were put to death by firing squad in two days' time. The SS literally wore out their rifle barrels in the process. Tepes not only shot Jews; he and his men were also charged with the duty of shooting any SS men who faltered during the slaughter. He received his training at the Border Police School Barracks in Pretzsch, Saxony. It consisted of a four-week course in rifle marksmanship and a series of lectures on the necessity of exterminating 'subhumans.' The course included actual killing of Russian prisoners of war."

"You aren't reading from the file," the girl said.

Jonas grimaced. "This one I know by heart," he said. "This one I've wanted to get for a long, long time. Somehow he slipped through the searchers' hands after the war. Probably because most of the people who could have recognized him were dead or locked away on the other side of the Iron Curtain. I know for a fact that sometime between the war's end and 1948 he escaped to Argentina. He was seen in the vicinity of the monastery of Mount Salvae in Belgrano in 1948. After that, he vanished."

"Thanks to U.S. Intelligence," Curt said. He paused before he spoke again. "I want you to know up front what's going to happen, Jonas. So there won't be any hassles further down the line. I have no intention of bringing this man Tepes to trial. He's not only protected by the CIA, but has his own private army surrounding him. If I can get to him, I'm going to wring out whatever information he has about my father's whereabouts in Paraguay, the Kameradenwerk defenses down there, and then I'm going to kill him."

It was the old man's turn to be silent. When he finally spoke, his voice was hard, his words clipped. "You know how I feel about executions without proper trials. There's no need to discuss that. And I know that I can't stop you from doing whatever you plan to do. I can and will intervene when it comes to innocent people. If you look at the photo again, you'll see two men on either side of Tepes. Those two were his closest companions during the war. They may be with him."

"The FBI man said Tepes had arranged for the CIA to smuggle some of his friends into the country, too," Sondra said.

"The one on the right of Tepes is Vlad Curoscu," Jonas went on as Curt once again examined the photograph. "He would be a very old man now. He was Tepes's early mentor, a confidant of Hora Sima, the national leader of the Iron Guard. The man on the left is Ante Palac. He is roughly the same age as Tepes. He'd be in his early sixties today. According to reports made during the war, Palac followed Tepes around like his pet dog. Both Curoscu and Palac participated in the Kiev massacre."

"I wish to hell you'd stayed in Italy," Curt said, passing the photo back to Arnstein. "It would've made everything so

59

much easier if you'd just sent the file to me by air express."

"Easier?"

"We don't know exactly what we're getting ourselves into," Curt told him. "We won't know until we arrive, and by then it might be too late. Keeping you out of trouble may not be possible."

"I can take care of myself, thank you," Jonas said. "Please, Sondra, turn on the radio. Let's have some music. Try to find a country western station."

For the next six hours Curt drove the Firebird due north on Interstate 75. There were plenty of country western stations. The drive itself was pretty boring, the landscape flat, rural, the highway straight as a string. Things changed after they crossed the bridge that connected Michigan and its Upper Peninsula. Plowed fields and pastures gave way to wooded hillsides and the road began to curve, winding its way between low hills.

It was a little after 6 P.M. when they arrived in the village of Harberstam. There was still enough daylight to see the city limits sign which put the population at 134. There was only one main street. It was lined on both sides with stores and shops. The rest of the town consisted of at most three dozen small houses scattered about on the heavily treed hills. The roads that ran in front of the houses had no sidewalks.

Curt parked near the town's only restaurant. It shared a one-story red-brick building with a barbershop. The crude, handpainted letters on the restaurant's front window said "U.P. Cafe."

"Looks real inviting, doesn't it?" he said, turning on his seat and winking at Sondra.

"I don't care how it looks," Jonas said. "I'm starving. Let's get something to eat."

"We can also probably pick up some information on our contact," Curt said as he opened the car door.

The three of them caught some hard stares when they walked into the cafe. The stares all came from a group of men sitting at the long counter. They were dressed in farm work clothes, their faces ruddy, seamed from exposure. They were all drinking Stroh's brand beer from bottles. In a back booth there was a family of tourists. The smallest child sat in a booster chair in the aisle.

"Let's sit by the window," Curt suggested.

"What is that smell?" Jonas asked, wrinkling up his nose as they sat down.

"There aren't any menus," Sondra said.

Curt pointed at the small chalkboard on an opposite wall. There were three things listed on it: grilled liver and onions, meatloaf, and tuna croquettes.

"You were right, Curt," Jonas said. "I should've stayed in Italy."

After a few minutes the waitress came over with full water glasses and silverware. She was in her middle fifties and wore her dyed black hair in a bouffant style that had gone out of fashion two decades before. "What can I get you folks tonight?" she asked.

They ordered from the chalkboard. It didn't take long for the food to arrive. Arnstein only ate the mixed vegetables. He refused to touch the instant mashed potatoes, fried onions or liver. The latter was the source of the pervasive unpleasant smell.

When the waitress returned to bring them the check, Curt said, "We're looking for a fellow who lives around here. Maybe you could tell us how to get in touch with him? His name is Zeb Mars."

"You're friends of his?" the waitress said.

"No, not exactly. We're up here for a little vacation. We've hired him to do some guiding for us. And we're renting a cabin of his."

The waitress gave him a curious look. "Renting Zeb's cabin?"

"That's what I said. Is something wrong?"

"No, of course not. It's just that, well, he doesn't have much in the way of visitors. Kind of a hermit, you know. I can't tell you where he is, but I can tell you how to get to his place."

Jaeger listened carefully to her directions, thanked her, and paid the check. As they left the cafe, the farmers at the counter stopped eating pickled bologna on crackers long enough to give them another round of hard stares. By the time Curt, Sondra and Jonas were back in the car, night was settling in fast. Jaeger turned on his headlights.

"Some real friendly people here," Sondra said.

"It isn't the kind of place that attracts a lot of strangers," Curt said, as he backed out of the parking place. "We don't have very far to go now, if what the waitress said was true."

He headed west until they came to the second crossroad, then turned right. The road paralleled a steep bluff for a mile or so before plunging into heavy woods. After another half-mile, the road became a dirt track, full of ruts and potholes. They wound around in the darkness for a couple of miles until the headlights picked up a plywood sign that had been nailed to the trunk of a maple tree. The sign said "Z. Mars."

Curt turned off the dirt road and up the narrow lane. The headlights swept across a monstrosity of a house, and he stopped the car.

"Don't tell me that's the place," Jonas said.

"It looks like it's straight out of Dog Patch," Sondra said.

Curt had to agree. It had once been a bungalow, but time and the elements had ruined it. Repairs to the structure had been made with items at hand: sheets of scrap tin, used lumber, even cardboard. All the window glass had been replaced by clear plastic which was taped and nailed in place. There were no lights on in the house, and the screen door sans screen, hung wide open.

"It doesn't look like anybody's home," Curt said, pulling the car up closer. "But we'd better get out and check." He took a flashlight from the glove compartment and led the way up the ramshackle stairs to the front porch.

"Hello?" he said, sticking his head in the open doorway. He flashed the light over the inside of the house, looking for an electric light switch. There was none, but a gas lantern sat in the middle of the cluttered dinette table.

"Just a minute," he told the others. He got the lantern going and turned it up full-blast. "Come on in."

"This place looks worse on the inside than it does on the outside," Sondra said.

"Hard to believe, but true," Jonas said.

"So the guy doesn't do much entertaining," Curt said, looking around at the piles of miscellaneous stuff. Fishing tackle and firearms were stacked in every corner. The dinette table held a strange mixture of things: fish hooks, feathers, squirrel tails, spools of tinsel, a half-empty pint bottle of bourbon, dishes from dinners long past. The other furniture was threadbare and shabby. The only pictures on the walls were advertisements ripped from outdoor magazines.

"I think this is what's called decorating on a shoestring," Jonas said.

"Or *with* shoestring," Sondra said.

The sound of a car pulling up the lane ended the speculation. "That's probably our man," Curt said, stepping around a pyramid of empty beer cans and out onto the front porch.

The car's headlights stopped abruptly about thirty feet from the house. Then a high power spotlight hit Curt full in the face. And a bull-horn-amplified voice said, "Hold it right there, mister. Don't move. Keep your hands in plain sight."

"What is it?" Sondra said, sticking her head out the door.

"The others in the house," said the bull-horn voice, "get out on the porch and don't try anything funny."

"Do as he says," Curt told them. He shuffled to the side, keeping his hands up.

When they were all in a line, the car door opened and a man started walking up to the house. For a second he stepped through the path of the spotlight and Curt could see that he was some kind of peace officer. He had a beige policeman's hat on and a heavy revolver in his right hand. The stairs creaked as the overweight officer climbed them.

"All right, what's going on here?" he demanded of Curt.

Jaeger noted that the pistol, a service Colt, was cocked and pointed at his midsection. It was no time for fun and games. "We dropped by to see Zeb Mars," Curt said. "He's supposed to do some guiding for us over the next couple of days."

"Doesn't look like Mars is around," the officer said. "What were you doing inside his house?"

"Waiting for him to come back," Curt said.

The officer eyed Jonas and the girl doubtfully. "We've had a few robberies around here lately. The locals don't lock their doors much. Sometimes strangers passing through can't resist the temptation."

"Have you seen the inside of this house?" Jonas said, leaning forward and reading the name etched into the little plastic nameplate pinned to the man's shirt pocket. "Deputy Dunlop, believe me, there's nothing in there that anybody in their right mind would want to steal."

"Maybe so, but I think all three of you ought to turn and face the wall. Put your hands up and spread your legs. Do it now."

As the officer slapped down Arnstein, Sondra said, "Look, we're just here to do a little camping and fishing, that's all."

Deputy Dunlop sized up her considerable curves, smirked, then began patting her down. "You don't feel like the outdoors type to me, honey."

Jaeger didn't like the way Deputy Dunlop was frisking the girl, and from the expression on Sondra's face, she liked it even less, but neither of them did or said anything. They couldn't stop the officer short of cleaning his clock. And cleaning his clock would jeopardize everything.

"When Mars gets here, he can settle the whole thing," Curt said as he, too, was searched for concealed weapons.

"Yeah, we'll just wait for old Mars," the officer said, stepping back while the others turned back around to face him. He still held the cocked pistol at waist level.

"You don't need that," Jaeger said, pointing at the gun.

"Maybe I don't and maybe I do. Like I said, we've had some trouble with strangers around here. There was a double murder awhile back. The first thing like that that's ever happened around here. It wasn't locals that got killed. It was a pair of TV news people who were snooping around, asking lots of questions. We found them in a ditch on the other side of town with their heads bashed in."

"Any suspects?" Curt said.

"No, not a one," the deputy admitted. "Still working on the case, of course, but the way I figure it, it was strangers killing strangers, then moving on. We'll never find out who did it. Kind of a sad state of affairs, isn't it?"

"Tragic," Curt answered.

The roar of another car made them all look down the lane. It raced up the drive and stopped beside the deputy's car. It was an ancient Willys pickup truck. The driver door opened and a tall, rangy man in a battered railroad engineer's cap got out and started for the house.

"What the hell's going on?" he said as

he walked up the stairs. His hair and beard were coppery red, his face long and cheekbones prominent.

"These folks claim to be clients of yours, Mars," the deputy said. "Marie over at the U.P. Cafe called me up after they got directions here from her. She thought they were suspicious. I caught them rummaging around inside your house. I thought they might be stealing from you."

"It's real kind of you and Marie to look after my property like that, Huey," Zeb Mars said. "Unexpected, but kind." He looked over Jaeger and the others, then smiled and put out his hand to Curt. "McFee has told me all about you. I'm glad to meet you and your friends."

As Curt shook his hand, the deputy said, "Well, I guess if everything's all right, I'll move on out."

"Good night, Huey," Mars said.

They waited until the sheriff's car had turned out of the lane and onto the dirt road before resuming their conversation.

"God, I thought we'd had it," Sondra said.

"If that tub of lard had gotten around to running our IDs through a computer, we would've had it," Curt said.

"You don't have to worry too much about computers up here," Mars said. "Things are primitive, like the deputy."

"He tried to lay a scare on us," Curt said. "Something about some snoopers who were murdered recently. He didn't say what they were snooping into."

"They were free-lance TV journalists looking into the current activities of Goga Tepes," Mars said. "It's a crime that's likely to go unsolved because the 'tub of lard,' as you call him, was undoubtedly one of the perpetrators. He and some of the boys from the monastery."

"The deputy is in the Iron Guard?" Jonas asked.

"Well, he went through some of the basic training, then washed out of the program. Couldn't keep his weight down. He also wasn't coordinated enough. He's like a lot of the people you find around here—not a member of Tepes's little clique, but would do anything to help its cause. You see, Goga Tepes is a kind of local hero. He calls himself a priest, though he has never been officially ordained, and this is a very religious community. Everybody knows his commitment to the retaking of the homeland from the communists. They know he does more than talk about it. He also has given good jobs to the men who've gone through his training program. They send nice fat checks back to the homefolks from Paraguay. So, Mr. Jaeger, when you fight Goga Tepes, you fight the whole town of Harberstam."

"Speaking of fighting," Curt said. "Just exactly what am I going to be fighting with? The only weapon I've got is a single-shot handgun."

"Come with me," Mars said, walking back down the stairs and over to the bed of his pickup. There was a pile of quartered firewood in it. He began shifting the chunks of wood until he uncovered a plastic tarpaulin. He turned back the tarpaulin and Curt shined his flashlight on a pair of M16A1 rifles equipped with bipods. Under the barrels of each was a curbed metal bracket that held a spherical projectile four inches in diameter. The white and black projectile was marked "HE."

"Rifleman's assault weapons," Jaeger said. "I thought RAWS they were still in the experimental stage. Where did you get them?"

"A buddy of mine in California is developing them," Mars said. "They're the ultimate street-fighting tool. Those projectiles are rocket-powered. They'll travel in a straight trajectory for up to two hundred meters. They'll blow a man-sized hole through eight inches of reinforced concrete."

"You're not going to make a whole lot of friends around here with those," Curt said.

"That's my problem. Come on, let's get you folks bedded down in the cabin. We're all going to be up real early tomorrow."

Chapter Four

Dick Welch lay on the narrow bed fully clothed, staring at the cracks in the ceiling. There were lots of cracks for him to stare at. It was a very old room. Electricity had been added to it long after this wing of the monastery had been built. All the electrical wires were visible. They ran across the middle of the ceiling to the overhead light. They ran along the baseboards to the wall sockets. The wires were encrusted with layer upon layer of thick paint. The last layer was cream-colored.

Welch's superiors at Langley had left it up to him to decide on-scene whether or not Goga Tepes should be terminated. He'd made his decision while they were eating dinner in the mess hall with the trainees. It wasn't a hard decision for him to make.

Before he'd left CIA headquarters for the monastery, Welch had studied all the available data on Tepes and his Iron Guard, as it existed in the present, as it had existed in the past. There was no doubt in his mind after he finished that reading that Tepes deserved to die for his crimes against humanity. The only question was whether anything could be salvaged from the company's considerable investment in him. Could the Rumanian be counted on to perform some future service to his adopted country, either here or abroad? Welch thought not.

In his view, Tepes's anticommunist stand was and always had been a front, a pose calculated to get him the support of the Rumanian-American locals and money from the federal government. Tepes would have used the Jews instead of the communists if he thought he could have gotten away with it. He was certainly much more familiar with using the Jews.

Welch was no stranger to killing, himself. During his ten years with the agency, he had been ordered to eliminate enemy agents both in the Far East and in Europe. A couple of times he had been forced by circumstances to do the deed up close, face-to-face. He still saw those faces in nightmares. Dick Welch was a killer when duty demanded it of him, but he took no pleasure from that sideline to his work. A creature like Goga Tepes, who had personally murdered thousands of noncombatants, women and babies, with no pangs of conscience, seemed to Welch something less than human.

The very atmosphere of the Upper Peninsula enclave gave Welch the creeps. The place seemed modeled after a hive or nest

of insects, wasps or hornets, all blindly
serving the whims of one master. Instead
of a queen, that master was a king, Goga
Tepes. From his reading, Welch knew that
in Rumanian the relationship was called
Capitanul, the cult of the leader. If the
sway Tepes held over his men at the monastery was disturbing, then the control he
wielded over those four thousand miles
away in Paraguay was truly frightening.
Welch comforted himself with a single
thought: the strength of Capitanul was
also its weakness. When the bullet passed
through Tepes's brain, his kingdom would
fall apart.

Welch's problem was how to terminate
the man and survive the act. To try and
shoot Tepes inside the monastery building
would be suicide. The man was always surrounded by legionnaires. Not that Welch
was overly concerned about taking out the
odd green shirt in the deal. Especially Palac
and Curoscu. Those two needed killing almost as much as Tepes. Welch kicked himself mentally for not seizing the ideal
opportunity when it had presented itself
earlier. He had been alone with Tepes in
the turret. A chance like that probably
wouldn't come again.

What he had to do was coax Tepes outside the compound, away from his ador-
ing troops. Perhaps he could get Tepes to
take him on a guided tour of the estate's
perimeter? Welch visualized the ideal sce-

nario. He and Tepes would ride in the back
seat of the Mercedes convertible, Palac and
Curoscu up front. The heavy caliber handgun would be inside Welch's coat. He could
turn as if looking at some point of in-
terest, lean against the big Rumanian
and actually jam the muzzle of the pistol
against the side of the man's chest. The
men in front would hear the muffled pop,
but by the time they realized its signifi-
cance it would be too late. He would shoot
the passenger through the back of the
head, then lean over the front seat, grab
the top of the steering wheel and fire again,
into the driver's neck.

From then on it would be no problem.
All he would have to do would be to push
the bodies in the front seat aside, slip behind the wheel, drive to the nearest gate,
shut off the power to the electric fence,
shoot the lock off the gate and drive away.
He could dump the corpses out in the boondocks, then ditch the car near the next
town.

He had been searched when he'd entered
the monastery, but his weapons hadn't been
discovered. They were concealed in separate
parts on his person and in his luggage.
He considered getting out the handgun
and having it ready, but decided against
it. He couldn't risk its being found before
he had a chance to use it.

Welch picked a crack in the ceiling at
random and began following its track with

his eyes, choosing new directions as it branched off, growing finer and finer. He felt very calm. When the time came to act, he would be precision itself.

Chapter Five

Deputy Huey Dunlop sat on a tree stump in the woods not a hundred feet from the front door of Zeb Mars's ramshackle house, thinking about powdered sugar-covered doughnut holes. He'd up and left a whole giant two-pound economy pack of them sitting on the back seat of his squad car. Sitting there, going to waste.

No, he told himself, this is a stakeout. I can't leave my post.

Except for the eerie, wavering lantern light coming from the unshaded windows of the house, the night was pitch-black. And it was cold. All of his insulating layers of fat didn't do him a bit of good, what with him just sitting there like a statue. But he didn't dare move around too much for fear of stumbling over something and blowing his surveillance of the newcomers.

He'd known right away that there was something wrong with them. And he'd always thought there was something wrong with Mars. It was his job to stay on top of things like that, to check up on his suspicions, so he'd driven his car out to the

81

main road, parked it, then walked back through the bush in the dark.

He put his hand down to his side and felt the hard grips of his service Colt. Just checking, he told himself. He eased the weapon in and out of its holster, limbering it up, making sure it would come to his hand in a flash if he needed it. Nobody was going to put one over on him.

A lanky shadow moved across one of the house's front windows. It was Mars. Mars getting himself a fresh bottle of booze. Deputy Dunlop shifted his buttocks on the stump, wishing to hell he'd thought to bring a pillow as well as the bag of doughnut holes.

Some people in Harberstam thought he had a second-rate job. He didn't think so. He believed a job was what you made of it. Not that it didn't hurt when he washed out of the monastery program, but he didn't let that get him get him down. He kept plugging away until he landed the deputy's badge. Now he had his own gun and a siren on his car, and if he wasn't quite good enough to go to Paraguay, he was plenty good enough to run errands, do dirty work and generally cover the skinny asses of the green shirts.

It wasn't his fault that he was slow on his feet or that he had a weight problem. It all came down to glands. And glands were something you were born with.

As he sat there, the two-pound bag of doughnut holes once again popped into his mind. How long, he wondered, would it take for him to trot over to the squad car and get them? Five, maybe ten minutes?

Deputy Dunlop shook himself. No, he told himself, he wasn't going to desert his post. He had will power. He'd show them all he could stick it out.

Chapter Six

Curt Jaeger jerked awake for the second time in less than an hour. Sweat dripped down the sides of his face, and his heart pounded. He'd had the bad dream again. The dream he'd been having ever since Schloss Grausheim, ever since he visited the gas chamber where his mother had been murdered.

He pushed the covers off and sat up on the cabin's lumpy couch. The images of the nightmare, sharp and clear, lingered in his mind. He had been looking through the viewport in the heavy metal door of the gas chamber, looking into the small, low-ceilinged room. On the other side of the glass was his mother as she appeared in photographs his foster parents had shown him. Except that she wasn't smiling serenely. She was terrified. She threw herself at the glass, begging him to help her escape. He couldn't open the door. He couldn't smash in the thick glass. He could only watch, his whole body trembling with impotent rage, while the chamber slowly filled with gas. His mother's face was obscured by the clouds of Zyklon B. Then he was looking at a face much like his own. A face with the same square, clefted chin, the same hard blue eyes. For a second he thought it had to be a reflection in the glass. Then the face smiled. It was his father's face, not his. Suddenly he felt a horrible pain in his throat and chest, and he realized that the gas was on his side of the view port, that he was the one who was trapped.

Jaeger shook his head to clear the dream from it, then got up from the couch and left the cabin. The night was cool and fresh, the air full of the smells of the woods. He saw that there was a light on in Mars's house, so he walked up the path to it.

Mars was sitting on a kitchen chair, his boots propped up on the littered table. He was drinking bourbon from the pint bottle.

"Mind if I join you?" Curt said.

The red-headed man waved him in. "Come on, sit down. Have some Dutch courage."

Jaeger sat down, but refused the liquor. "That isn't why you're drinking, is it?"

Mars eyed the level of the fluid in the bottle. "I've never been afraid of a fight. I'm drinking because I always drink. Because I like it. You don't have to worry about my getting drunk on you. That hasn't happened for years."

"I've got to ask you something that's been bothering me," Curt said.

"Shoot."

"You've lived here a long time. After I

break into the monastery and do my thing, your name is going to be mud around here. How're you going to handle that?"

Mars smiled. "My name has always been mud around here," he said. "You see, I'm not a Rumanian. Most people in these parts are. They tolerate me because I'm a loner and stay out of their way. I can be a loner anyplace."

"You mean you intend to leave?"

Mars took a pull on the bottle, swallowed, grimaced. "I've been thinking about it for quite a while. I've been thinking about Wyoming. It's got good hunting and fishing. And there aren't any war criminals, so far as I know."

"Wyoming sounds okay."

"I'm not risking anything in this, except my life," Mars said. "And I figure risk is worth it. I spent a lot of years in the Bureau chasing down counterfeiters and stolen cars. I never had the chance to get a mass murderer. It sounds like something to shoot for, doesn't it?"

Jaeger didn't answer. He knew that Mars was no idiot. That the ex-FBI man was aware of the odds stacked against them. They had to penetrate a defensive stronghold and overcome vastly superior odds. If they succeeded, they would have the CIA to reckon with. If they succeeded, they'd have to find a hole and crawl into it.

Mars nursed the bottle along for a couple of hours, and they talked about other things. About the FBI, J. Edgar Hoover, and Special Agent-in-Charge McFee. Mars had little respect for the first, less for the second, but a genuine admiration for the third. Curt agreed with him about McFee.

Finally, Mars chucked the empty bottle at the already overflowing trash can and got up. He stretched, then said, "Better go down and wake up your friends. I'll round up something for us to eat. I want to be moving before first light."

When Curt returned with Sondra and Jonas, the dinette table had been cleared and it was set with chipped plates and mismatched silverware. Mars served them eggs and bacon, and fresh raspberries for their cereal. He did not eat, himself, but drank mug after mug of steaming black coffee.

"We'd better go over the plan now," he said. "This is just going to be a reconnoiter trip to give you an idea of the layout. Afterwards, we'll regroup back here and decide how we want to handle the seige."

"Understood," Curt said.

"I've done some snooping in the area since I heard from McFee," Mars said. "I'm going to take you through the woods to an overlook. The main buildings are about half a mile from that point. We've got to be very quiet, though, because Tepes keeps guard dogs. Also, I should warn you the exterior fence is electrified."

"You've got binoculars?" Sondra asked.

"Enough for all of us," Mars said. "There

is one other thing that we should discuss, though."

"What's that?" Jonas said.

"We aren't going to be able to take any weapons with us this time."

"No weapons?" Sondra said. "Considering what happened to those reporters, isn't that taking a bit of an unnecessary risk?"

"No, it's absolutely necessary," Mars told her. "If we have guns and get caught near the monastery there'll be a fire fight. And it'll be on their terms. We'll have blown the element of surprise, which is probably the only thing we've got on our side. Without guns, you're just a group of out-of-state tourists I'm taking on a nature walk."

"It makes sense," Jonas said.

"I agree," said Curt.

"I don't like it," Sondra told them. "But I guess we have no choice."

After breakfast, they packed up a couple of knapsacks with binoculars, sketch pads and cameras. When they left the house, it was still pitch black outside.

Mars took the lead, moving slowly, carefully down a narrow lane through the pine trees. He was followed by Sondra, then Jonas, with Curt bringing up the rear. Mars held a flashlight but used it sparingly, only when there was some obstacle those behind him might stumble over.

They crossed a creek and began climbing up a heavily forested slope. Curt pushed Jonas from behind, helping him up when the going got really rough. They stopped to rest at the summit. Above them, the sky was full of stars; the moon had long since set.

"How much farther?" Jonas asked softly.

"Not far," Mars told him. "We have to circle the rim of this hill and then we're there."

It sounded easier than it was. The bedrock of the hill was exposed, and they had to clamber over the outcrops. By the time they reached their destination the night was beginning to fade.

"That's the monastery, there," Mars said, pointing across the valley to the bright pinpoints of light.

"It looks bigger than I'd expected," Curt said.

"Yeah, it's going to be a tough nut to crack."

They waited out the minutes until the sun was about to come up, until they could see without straining, then all four of them began surveying the scene with binoculars.

Inside the compound, men were already moving around. Some were tending the dogs, some doing warm-up exercises.

"As you can see," Mars said, "the main building is a kind of hodgepodge affair."

"Horseshoe-shaped," Sondra said.

"It looks like a barracks," Curt said.

"The center building was there first, the wings added later by Tepes," Mars said. "You can see the exterior fence runs around the entire perimeter. There are gates every fifty yards or so, all padlocked and electrified. Inside the perimeter is a fenced dog run."

"Look at all those light poles," Jonas said.

"They can really crank up the candle power if they want to," Mars said.

"Is that a firing range over there?" Sondra said, pointing to the north along the line of the hill they were sitting on.

"Yes," Mars said. "And they practice with some heavy stuff, too. They've got automatic weapons and antitank gear. When they really get it going, it sounds like World War III."

"See that stone fence?" Jaeger said. "It runs right up against that grove of trees. And stops within what looks like seventy yards of the main building. That might be our way in."

"I think you're right," Mars said. "It would give us solid cover. Otherwise, we'd be running from light pole to light pole."

"Is there any way we could get a better look at it?" Curt said. "I'd like to see if we're going to have any major problems reaching it."

"If we walk down the hill and parallel the fence into the woods we should be able to tell. Tepes and his men like to play games in there, though. Maybe Sondra and Jonas would be better off staying here?"

"I know I would," Jonas said. "If I walk down this hill, I'm going to have to climb up it again, and that's something I don't want to do, ever."

"I don't mind," Sondra said. "We can sketch the defenses."

"Yeah. And Jonas, you should keep an eye out for any of the men we're after," Curt said. "Watch where they go, where they come from."

"Of course," the old man said.

"Most important of all," Mars said, "stay low and keep quiet. Understand?"

Sondra and Jonas nodded.

"All right, let's go," Mars said, taking the lead again.

Curt followed him down the hill. They moved at a much faster pace than before, jumping from rock to rock, then running down the heavily treed slope. As fast as they moved, they made very little noise.

When Mars and Jaeger reached the bottom of the hill, they began working their way through the thicket of pines, moving toward the narrow band of cleared ground that separated the woods from the electrified fence. They were no more than four feet from the edge of the tree line when Mars suddenly stopped short, then slowly dropped to his stomach on the ground.

He did not have to gesture for Curt to do the same. Jaeger had already seen the movement through the screen of pine boughs, movement on the far side of the fence. Not forty feet away, two men in dark green shirts were walking toward them. At their sides, held in check by heavy leads, were a pair of big Alsatian dogs.

Jaeger carefully crawled over the carpet of pine needles to where Mars lay.

The red-haired man whispered in his ear. "We have to sit tight. If we try and make a break for it, those dogs will hear us. There's a gate just over there to the left."

Jaeger nodded. No further explanation was needed. If he and Mars were discovered, the men in green could open the gate and turn the dogs loose. A two-legged animal running uphill against a four-legged one didn't stand a chance in hell.

Curt watched grimly, barely breathing as the two Iron Guardists moved closer. The crack of a twig under his legs, a sudden shift in the wind that brought their scent to the dogs, and the battle would be over before it had begun.

Chapter Seven

Jonas Arnstein lowered his binoculars. "I think I see Tepes," he said. "Just coming out of the main building on the left."

Sondra raised her field glasses and took in the scene. There was no mistaking the lord of the manor. For one thing, the moment he set foot in the yard, all the rugged young men in green shirts went to rigid attention. For another, he towered over the rest of them, and particularly over the rotund little fellow scuttling along at his heels.

"I'd bet anything that the fat one behind him is Ante Palac," Jonas said.

"You'd win," said a familiar voice to the rear and above them.

As Sondra and Jonas turned, Deputy Huey Dunlop stepped out from behind a rock outcrop. He was smiling, and he had his service Colt in his hand. He was not alone. With him were four of the men in green, armed with HK assault rifles.

"What're the guns for?" Sondra said indignantly.

"What're the binoculars for?" the deputy

said. "You wouldn't be a pair of snoopers, would you? Not after I went and told you what happened to the last pair of those we found hereabouts?"

"There's no law against having a pair of binoculars, is there, officer?" Jonas said. "And we aren't trespassing, are we?"

"I don't know what you are, mister, but I think Goga Tepes will be able to find out real quick. He has a knack for getting answers out of people. Now, let's move on along and see if we can't find your two friends. I know Tepes will want to talk to them, too."

It was clear to Sondra that she couldn't do anything to save either herself or Jonas, but she could prevent Curt and Mars from being captured. As the men approached, she turned as if to put her binoculars down in the knapsack, then jumped over the rock ledge, dropping out of sight of her would-be captors.

"Get her!" the deputy shouted.

Sondra raced down the hill, slipping, sliding through piles of leaves, running away from Curt and Mars.

Above her on the hillside she could hear the men crashing through the undergrowth. Then she came to the electric fence and there was only one direction she could run. The men in green were shouting to each other, and their shouting alerted the watchdogs, who began barking furiously. At least Jaeger and Mars would know that something bad was going down.

Then, ahead of her, a man slid down a gulley and stopped, blocking her way. She didn't try to go around. She ran right for him. And when he put out his hands to grab her, she launched herself at him, headfirst. Like a defensive tackle, she rammed into the man's gut. He groaned as the wind was knocked out of him, as he was driven over onto his back. Unlike a defensive tackle, Sondra had no helmet to protect her head from the impact. She fell to the ground on top of her victim, momentarily stunned, then rolled away, fighting to clear her head. She pushed up to her feet, took a shaky step or two, then fell again. By the time she recovered fully it was too late. She was surrounded.

"Well, you sure can run, honey," Deputy Dunlop said, panting as he joined the younger, lighter, faster men who'd cornered her. He had Jonas by the arm, and the Colt was still in his hand. "Go ahead, grab her and let's get back to the monastery. Her friends are long gone by now."

Two of the men in green approached Sondra. They approached warily, from opposite sides.

"Go on, she ain't gonna bite," the deputy chided.

When the man on her left lunged, Sondra ducked and pivoted. The would-be grabber brushed past her, but not before she snapped a hard sidekick behind his left knee. He went down, howling.

The other man didn't mess around after

seeing what had happened to his partner. He came at her swinging with both hands. Expertly, the black-haired girl blocked and parried the flurry of blows, turning them out, up, down, away from their intended targets. Then she drop-kicked him right on the point of the chin. It was a full-power kick, with lots of snap at the finish. It straightened the guy upright, made his teeth clack together, and then he was going over backwards, out cold before he hit the ground.

"Har, har," Deputy Dunlop said. "I think the babe likes to wrestle. Wanna wrestle with me, too, honey?"

Sondra wiped the sweat from her forehead and waved him on.

Dunlop grinned at her, then for the benefit of the others as well as her, he said, "You know what happens if you lose, don't you? If I pin you? Har, har. If I pin you, I'm gonna take you. Sound like fun?"

The black-haired girl shot a quick glance behind her, measuring the distance between herself and the electric fence. Then she was moving, shifting from side to side as the fat man stepped closer. "Hold my gun," he said, handing it to the nearest green shirt. "I'm gonna need two hands for what she's got under that sweater."

When the deputy charged, Sondra easily evaded him. She fired off a hard kick into his broad behind. His forward momentum and the force of the blow sent him to his knees in the leaves.

"Damn!" he said, getting up slowly. "Damn, you're going to pay for that, honey. And I'm going to love making you pay."

With that, he whirled and dove for her ankles. She jumped but he got a hand on her right foot and she went down on her back hard.

"Gotcha!" he said, pulling himself up along her legs. His eyes were on the prizes under her sweater. It was the wrong place to be looking.

Sondra cut loose with a savage combination to his head. Not just her fists, but elbows and forearms.

The deputy raised up, trying to protect his face with his hands. She punched right through his guard and his nose cracked under her fist.

"Jesus!" he wailed, rolling off her, clutching at his face. Tears poured down his fat cheeks, blood poured onto his uniform. He pulled a big white handkerchief from his back pocket and held it to his nose. "You bitch!" he said. clambering to his feet. "I'll blow your fucking head off! Give me my gun!"

The green shirt who held his service revolver started to laugh. Then all the others joined in.

"My gun!" the deputy demanded.

"Sure," the green shirt said. He flipped open the cylinder and dumped the bullets into his palm. He tossed the empty gun to Dunlop and put the bullets into his pocket.

"Asshole," the deputy growled, reaching

around to take a bullet from the loops on the side of his holster belt.

"I wouldn't do that if I were you, Huey," the green shirt said.

"You ain't me," Deputy Dunlop said, pushing the live round into the cylinder with his thumb, then snapping the cylinder closed.

"Yeah, I'm not stupid."

Dunlop cocked back the pistol's hammer and aimed at the center of Sondra's face. As he did so, a wicked smile spread across his mouth.

"I'm not going to be the one to deprive our leader of the chance to meet such a pretty little lady," the green shirt said.

The deputy's smile vanished at once. The man in the green shirt had pushed the right button. The fear button. "But dammit, she broke my goddam nose!" Dunlop whined.

"Hey, you do what you have to do, Huey."

"Son of a bitch!" Deputy Dunlop snarled. He eased down the hammer with his thumb and then jammed the weapon back into its holster. To Sondra he said, "There are a lot worse things then a bullet in the head, honey. And you're going to learn that firsthand."

He grabbed Jonas by the shoulder and pushed him ahead. "Move!" he said. "Both of you!"

The entire group walked along the fence until they came to a padlocked gate. Another green shirt was waiting for them on the other side. He shut off the power to the fence at a switchbox and unlocked the gate.

Sondra and Jonas walked through along with their escort. The gate was locked after them, and the power switched on. As they passed the fenced dog run, a Doberman hurled himself at them, bulging the wire, then gnawing it ferociously with his teeth.

"I think he likes you," Deputy Dunlop said.

Sondra and Jonas said nothing, but just kept on walking in the direction of the main building. As they approached the compound yard, the men in green standing around all gathered for a good look at what had been caught. They quickly stepped aside when Tepes himself burst onto the scene.

"What is this?" he demanded. "Who are they?"

"Found them up on the ridge with binoculars," Deputy Dunlop said.

Tepes eyed his swollen nose and bloody handkerchief. "Did the old bastard do that to you?"

"I . . . uhh . . fell," the fat officer said.

Tepes grimaced at him.

"We were just doing some bird watching," Jonas said. "We didn't realize we were doing anything wrong."

"Where do I know you from?" Tepes said, leaning down and staring into Jonas's face.

Arnstein stared back.

"You're a Jew, aren't you?"

"That's no more a crime in this country than bird-watching."

"Not just any Jew. I've seen you. I've seen your picture." Tepes snapped his fingers. "Aha!" he said. "You're Arnstein. Arnstein, the world-famous Nazi-hunter. The man who gets his photo in all the magazines. The one who makes a lot of noise but gets no results."

Arnstein said nothing.

"Gentlemen," Tepes said, "come closer, take a good look at this dangerous fellow, the little dried-up old Jew who wants to destroy the Kameradenwerk."

The men in the green shirts moved in closer, snickering and making rude jokes.

"Well, Arnstein," Tepes said, "it looks like your days of glory are over." He looked at Sondra, appraising her face and figure. "And for your Jewess, too."

"There were two others with them," Deputy Dunlop said. "Two men. One of them was Zeb Mars, the hermit who lives on the far side of the woods. They ran when we captured the old man and the girl."

"Take two or three men and go over to Mars's shack," Tepes told him. "If they come back, kill them."

"You'll never get away with this," Jonas said.

"Oh, I think I will," Tepes said. He looked at Sondra again, his gaze lingering this time on her statuesque curves. "I have something very special for you," he said, reaching out to touch her pale cheek.

She flinched and moved out of his reach.

"You're a pig," Jonas said.

Tepes clucked his tongue at him. "Don't worry, Arnstein, I'll let you watch the whole thing. Why, it'll be just like the good old days, won't it?"

"What do you mean?"

"The good old days in the death camp," he said, grabbing hold of Arnstein's right arm, pushing the sleeve up and turning it so that the blue tattoo showed. "You must have done a lot of watching there. You watched while thousands of others died. I wonder how that came to be?"

Jonas twisted out of the big man's grip.

"How did you manage to survive? Did you carry corpses to the crematoria? Or did you rob your own dead for the Reich?"

Arnstein stiffened as if struck. Trembling with rage, he spit into Goga Tepes's face.

Tepes wiped the saliva away with his hand and waved back his legionnaires. Then he hit the old man full in the face, knocking him down.

"Leave him alone!" Sondra said, stepping between Tepes and his victim. She assumed a fighting stance.

"You're seriously undergunned," Tepes said, drawing his hogleg .44 Magnum from its holster. He cocked it and pointed it between Sondra's breasts. "Help the old man up and come along quietly, or your lives are going to end out here in the dirt."

Sondra helped Jonas to his feet, and the two of them went along quietly into the monastery.

Chapter Eight

Dick Welch was just getting dressed when he heard laughter in the compound yard. He walked to his bedroom window and looked down. As he watched, Goga Tepes knocked an old man, a stranger, to the ground. There was a girl, too, a very pretty black-haired girl.

Because the window was closed, because he didn't open it, not wanting to attract attention to himself, he couldn't make out the conversation that ensued between the tall Rumanian and his unwilling guests. One gesture, however, was worth a thousand words. The gesture in this case being the pulling of a pistol. At gunpoint the old man and the girl were forced to march into the main building.

As Welch turned away from the window, his guts tightened into a cold, hard knot. He knew everything about Goga Tepes. He knew about Einsatzgruppe "D" and he knew about the more recent crimes, including the double murder of the freelance journalists digging into Tepes's Nazi past. The old man and the girl were victims-to-be, of that there could be no doubt. The only question was whether Welch would permit more murder to happen when he had the power to stop it.

He sat down on the edge of his bed and put his face into his hands. If he played it safe, let the newcomers meet their fate, he could stick to his original plan, pick his time and place, and be reasonably sure of getting out with a whole skin. He couldn't play it safe, though, and keep any self-respect. That Tepes was still alive was his responsibility. If he allowed the man to survive long enough to kill two more people, then their blood would be on his hands, too.

His plan to isolate Tepes outside the compound had to be junked. The killing would have to be done in the presence of the green shirts. That meant his first line of offense couldn't be the high-power automatic pistol hidden among his belongings.

He reached over to the nightstand by the bed and picked up his fountain pen. It was gold-plated and inscribed with his name. He unscrewed the cap, then unscrewed the pen's barrel, removing the ink cartridge. Setting the dismantled pen on the little table, he took off his right shoe and twisted the heel to the side, revealing a small compartment. Inside the compartment, wrapped in tissue paper, was another cartridge for the pen and a replacement tip section. He put the old parts in his heel and assembled the pen with the new. It would not write now, but it would kill, silently, effectively. The new cartridge contained a quarter cc of highly toxic cyanide liquid under pressure. When the pen's flow lever was activated, it would shoot a super-fine mist of the deadly fluid through its new tip. When the tiny droplets were inhaled, they surged into the victim's system through exposed capillaries inside the nose and lungs. Death occurred within seconds, and it had all the appearance of being a heart attack.

Welch had been thoroughly schooled in the use of the poison pen. He knew its effective range and the danger it presented to the user. He took a kleenex from the pack he traveled with and tore off two small sections, rolling them individually into a pair of hard little balls. He then carefully fitted them inside his nostrils. If he didn't breathe through his mouth he was safe from the spray, which dissipated rapidly after it was shot.

He slipped the pen into his shirt pocket. As he did so, he ran the device's operating instructions through his mind. Get within three feet of the victim, aim the pen's tip at the center of the face, hold your breath, fire, and continue holding your breath through a count of 30, unless of course you have the opportunity to turn and run. Welch gritted his teeth. He knew he wouldn't have a chance to run. He knew he'd be damned lucky to fire the pen without being seen by one of Tepes's ever-present hangers-on. If he was seen he had to be ready with something more than a gold fountain pen.

He put his shoe back on and got his suitcase out from under the bed. He laid it on the bed and opened it, pulling out the inner fabric liner, then cracking what appeared to be a solid plastic seam that ran around the inside of the suitcase lid. The seam cracked easily, and he lifted out the false panel. Under it, embedded in protective foam, was a Smith and Wesson Model 59 automatic pistol in 9mm with two loaded fourteen-round clips.

He picked up the heavy pistol and snapped a clip into its butt, then jacked a live round under the hammer. He let the hammer down carefully and took a roll of adhesive tape from his shaving kit. He depressed the grip safety, then wound tape around the grip. The pistol had to go off even if he didn't have a good hold on it. There wasn't going to be time to take an Olympic stance if he had to use it.

He slipped the extra clip into his pants pocket, then cocked the Smith and Wesson and tucked it into his waistband behind his back so that the cold muzzle nestled between his buttocks. He put on his suit coat and checked himself out in the mirror, looking for a telltale bulge beneath the back of the coat. The gun was visible only when he buttoned up the jacket, so he left it unbuttoned.

A half-dozen times in front of the mirror he practiced drawing the cocked, loaded, safety-less pistol. It was hard as hell. He couldn't do it very quickly, not without the risk of putting a second hole in his ass. The only way to handle the problem was to avoid the quick-draw grab manuever altogether. If he casually slipped his hand inside his open jacket, as if to massage an ache in his back, he could get his fingers around the pistol grip. Once he had hold of the gun, it was easy to whip it out at something approaching top speed.

Welch replaced the automatic in his waistband and examined his face in the mirror's reflection. He looked old, overweight and tired. The sense of calm he'd felt before was gone. None of that mattered. Welch adjusted the front of his coat, straightened his tie, and headed for the door.

Chapter Nine

When all the shouting started, Curt thought
he and Mars had been discovered. It quickly
became clear to him, however, that that
wasn't the case. The men in green shirts
and dogs that had them pinned down
weren't coming toward them. They were
running away, running in the direction
Curt and Mars had come from. The direction of Sondra and Jonas.

Jaeger was up and moving at once. This
time Mars was the one bringing up the rear.
The sandy-haired ex-Green Beret sprinted
up the slope until he hit the much steeper
rock outcropping. Then it was hand over
hand and slow going. Sweat bathed his
face and back, his muscles threatened to
cramp up, but he kept on going.

As he scampered over the rim of the
ridge and once again broke into a run,
he cursed himself for not insisting that
they bring at least one weapon. Mars was
right on his heels, matching him step for
step.

When they reached the spot where they'd
left the old man and the girl, there was no

one around. Not even a sign of their having been there.

"Are you sure this is it?" Jaeger said. "Couldn't it be further on?"

Mars looked across the meadowland to the monastery to check their position. What he saw marching over the field made him swear aloud.

Curt looked, too. He said nothing. His friends were surrounded by men in green, being led at gunpoint to the compound. It was too late to swear. Too late for recriminations about not having brought guns along. There was no way guns would help in this situation. Jonas and Sondra were already too far away.

"All right," Mars said, "they're in a tight spot. There's no denying it. But so are we. Take a look through these."

Curt took the proffered binoculars. He watched the gathering in the yard.

"The fat man in the sheriff's uniform," Mars said. "Deputy Dunlop, remember?"

"I remember."

"He must've followed us from the cabin and used his walkie talkie to call in reinforcements from the monastery. He knows that we're still on the loose. He's going to be after us."

"I'm not worried about that," Curt said. "But our only chance to help Sondra and Jonas is to get hold of your arms cache. Maybe the fat man has already put a guard on your cabin. It's bound to occur to him sooner or later. We'd better get a move on."

"Right," Mars said, taking the lead.

They ran at an even pace down the hill and along the edge of the fence. When they came to the path leading to Mars's cabin, they cut their speed in half.

"I doubt that they'd bother to set up an ambush in here," Mars said, "but it wouldn't hurt to move more cautiously."

Curt agreed on all counts. The woods were too thick for an ambush. Too many tree trunks too close to the path. Ambushers would have to be standing with their gun muzzles even with the edge of the foliage in order to insure a clear shot. It was the kind of risk the Kameraden were not known for.

About a hundred yards from the cabin, Mars stopped and pushed aside a tree branch. "Deer trail," he said softly, pointing at the hidden pathway.

Curt followed the red-haired man through the opening in the brush, then watched as Mars dropped to all fours and scuttled off into the boondocks. Mighty small goddam deer, he thought as he got down on his hands and knees and crawled after the ex-FBI man.

A hundred yards is a long way when you're traveling on all fours. Jaeger couldn't nudge Mars to hurry up because he could barely keep up with the man. They definitely would have made much better time on the main path, but the main path was what the green shirts would be watching.

When Mars stopped again, it was at the base of a big pine tree with branches that brushed the ground. Curt moved in alongside him.

"Well?" Curt said.

"I don't see anybody," Mars answered.

Jaeger surveyed the clapboard house. There was no one on the porch, no movement inside, no one standing in the yard. "Me, either. Let's do it!"

But as Mars pushed forward, fending away a branch with both hands, the sound of engines racing, roaring, echoed through the woods. Curt caught Mars by the belt and held him back.

They both watched as the deputy sheriff's car and a battered old stake truck pulled up into Mars's front yard. There were three men in the car and another six in the truck. They were all armed.

"Dammit," Mars muttered. "Another two minutes and we could've gotten to my Jeep."

"Yeah, I know," Curt said. He watched as the deputy sheriff ordered the men in green around. Obviously the fat man got a real kick out of being in command for a change. The men in green didn't seem to appreciate it the way he did, though. They did what he said, taking up positions on the porch, in the house and the yard, but when his back was turned they made sullen faces.

Jaeger slumped back against the trunk of the tree. Time was slipping away. Jonas and Sondra were in mortal danger. He had to do something fast. If the weapons in the Jeep were inaccessible, there was still the gun in the trunk of the rented Firebird. Jaeger frowned when he thought of it. In this situation it was not the kind of piece he would have picked. It only held one shot.

"Look," he said to Mars, "I think I can work my way around to the Firebird. If I can get the trunk open without waking up those guys, there's a pistol inside. We use it to get a couple of their HK's, then clean up. Are you game?"

"What other choice have we?"

"Follow me, then," Jaeger said, turning back into the undergrowth.

He took care not to rustle any branches or snap any twigs, but he moved quickly, circling the house and coming up behind the parked Firebird. The nearest sentry was leaning against the cabin's rock chimney, his submachine gun held casually in the crook of his arm.

While Mars watched the lookout, Curt fitted the key to the trunk lock, opened it, then lifted the lid just enough to get his hand inside. His fingers found the grips of his kit bag. He had to raise the lid a bit to get the bag out. He then pushed the trunk lid down until the catch just clicked.

Mars looked away from his man for a second, watching as Jaeger took from the bag an oblong wrapped in soft cloth. When Curt unwrapped the pistol, Mars did a double-take. It was a strange-looking weapon, all right. Built on a rifle bolt action, its overall length was under fifteen inches. The stock that held the action was T-shaped, the pistol grip roughly in the center, the bolt and receiver hanging back over the wrist of the shooter. Attached to the receiver was a long black telescopic sight.

Curt carefully opened the action and took a single .308 Winchester round from the kit bag. He slipped it into the chamber, shoved the bolt home and locked it down.

Mars held up one finger, his expression one of exasperation and astonishment. One finger meaning "Only one shot?!"

Curt nodded grimly. One shot would have to do.

They backed up into the bushes and held a whispered conference.

"You're not going to like what I'm about to suggest," Curt said.

"Yeah, I know. What is it?"

Jaeger drew a rectangle with his finger in the dirt. He put dots where each of the men in green were standing. There were five dots outside the box, four inside. He pointed at the dot that represented the man by the chimney.

"If you were in position to take this guy out, say in a line with the edge of the house, none of the other soldiers could see you make your move."

"Right."

"So, you get in position while I stay here, keeping the target in my sights. When you make your move on him, he's going to react. When he does, as soon as he starts to swing on you, I'm going to cut loose with this." He patted the handgun. "By the time you reach him he's not going to be in any shape to object to your taking his submachine gun. You do know how to operate an HK?"

Mars nodded. "Okay, I get the gun, but the others will have heard the shot. I'm going to have guys in green crawling all over me."

Curt reached into his shirt pocket and picked out another .308 Winchester round. "I'm fairly quick when it comes to reloading. If you can keep them out of your face, I should be able to keep them off your back. At least long enough to drop another one and get hold of an HK for me to use. After that, it's just a matter of playing it by ear."

"Your plan stinks," Mars said. "But I can't come up with anything better."

"When I see him move," Curt said, "I'm going to shoot. You'd better have a head of steam worked up when you bust out of the bush."

"Don't miss," Mars said. He slipped off into the trees.

Jaeger moved forward, parting the foliage until he had a clear shot at the sentry. He assumed the Creedmoor position, flat on his back, the handgun resting on the outside of his right leg at shin height, his head raised, propped up by his left arm. It was a position for shooting at small targets at long distances. In this case, the target was only forty feet away. Curt was using the Creedmoor because from it he could roll to his feet very quickly.

He lined the crosshairs up on the lookout's chest, aiming for the third button on his shirt. The scope's field of vision was wide enough so he could also see the man's face. When the head jerked around to the left, Curt squeezed off the shot. The handgun roared, bucking hard and high against his solid grip.

The special, aluminum-jacketed, soft-lead slug slammed the sentry back against the chimney, his arms flying wide, the HK submachine gun flying due north. Jaeger had no doubt that the man was dead. The hole the bullet had made was right over his heart. As it passed through his body, the slug would have mushroomed, expanding to four times its entry diameter, cutting a cone shaped wound, leaving a fist-sized exit in his back.

Curt jacked open the pistol's bolt, dropped in a second round and shoved it home. As he locked down the bolt, he was already shifting position so he could cover Mars's rear.

The red-headed man was forced to do an abrupt change of direction in order to follow the flying submachine gun. In the process he slipped to his knees. He didn't

wait to regain his feet; he dove for the
gun. Cracking back the weapon's bolt, flip-
ping off the safety, he rolled for the side
of the house. A trail of hot slugs stitched
through the pine needles where he had
just been. Mars answered fire, leaning out
around the chimney. His target had already ducked behind the corner of the
building, and that was where Mars aimed.
He cut loose a stuttering ten-round burst
that chewed the clapboard siding to splin-
ters. It also chewed the shooter to splin-
ters. He toppled sideways to the dirt, his
head and face a wreck.

Curt wasn't paying any attention to what
Mars was doing. He had drawn a bead on
the edge of the cabin's long wood pile. A
face popped into his vision frame. An in-
tent, flushed face. Curt waited until the
man was halfway along the woodpile, holding the sight steady on the right temple,
then tightened down on the hair-set trigger. The gun boomed and reared. The least
Jaeger could do was to provide a painless
end. And that's what he did. There can be
no pain where there is no brain.

Curt rolled to his feet and dashed for
the fallen HK. He got it up and around
just as a man in green ran around the
corner of the building. The man in green
was ready to fire; Curt was not. He feinted
with his head, then spun away in the opposite direction, slapping back the submachine gun bolt as he did so. The man in
green fired into the space where Curt had

been. Curt on the other hand swept his flame-belching muzzle in a neat arc that transected the green man's torso. The impact of half a dozen 9-mm slugs knocked him flat on his back. He did not get up. He just lay there and twitched.

"Got it!" Jaeger shouted at top volume.

A burst of submachine gun fire from the other side of the house told him that Mars was still in business. It was time to play it by ear. And that's exactly what Curt did. He stopped and listened very carefully. He could hear footsteps on the rickety porch that was just around the corner of the house from him. The men inside had come out, but seeing how their comrades had disappeared, they had second thoughts about barging right after them.

Curt looked back over his shoulder at the rock chimney. It was made of big round stones stuck together in a cement matrix. There wasn't time to ponder over the decision. He put the handgun down beside the woodpile. There was only time to act. Jaeger ran to the chimney and started climbing it, the HK over his arm on its shoulder sling. If any one had chosen that particular moment to stick their head around the corner of the cabin, he would have been dead meat, so he didn't dawdle. He stepped onto the roof and swung the HK back into his hands.

The roof didn't look in much better shape than the front porch. He was betting his life that it was.

"Go for it, Mars!" he shouted over his shoulder, then he broke into a helter-skelter run along the spine of the roof. He skidded down the front slope and jumped onto the porch roof with both feet. The roof didn't hold his weight for more than a second. It gave way under him, the supporting posts slipping aside, the whole structure crashing down on the men in green beneath it. There were screams at first and a great cloud of dust as Curt hit and rolled away from the collapse. He turned, kneeling, and fired into the jumble of timber and scrap sheet metal. Mars rounded the corner from the other side and added his fire to Curt's. The screams abruptly stopped.

At the other end of the house, however, there was a tinkling of broken glass.

Jaeger and Mars ran in opposite directions, each one taking a different side of the house. Curt caught a glimpse of a plump figure escaping around the corner. Almost at once there came a horrendous burst of fire. And the plump figure was flung back into his sight. Rubbery legged, limp-armed, it toppled over onto its back. Deputy Dunlop had written his last parking ticket.

Mars stepped into view, his HK still smoking. He shook his head and wiped his face with his hand. "The dumb bastard almost ran me down. He caught it point-blank."

"I'll say," Curt agreed. The deputy's shirt was on fire.

"What now?" Mars asked.

"Got another idea you're not going to like."

"Jesus!"

"Let's clear some of the roof off the boys on the porch. We may find a use for a couple of uniforms."

Getting the roof off was less of a chore than getting the uniforms on. Most of them were more red than green. Jaeger and Mars stripped down right there and put on the clothes that were the least messed up.

"Now for the M16s," Mars said.

He and Curt pushed aside the wood in the Jeep's bed and retrieved the automatic weapons and RAW attachments.

"There's two more of these RAW gizmos in the pack, there," Mars said, pointing at a knapsack still partially buried.

Curt pulled the pack free and slung it over his arm.

"How're we going to do this?" Mars said.

"Let's go back up the ridge where we were before," Jaeger said. "We've got to find out what their alert status is."

Curt paused to pick up his special handgun and slipped it into the pack, then trotted after Mars, who was already disappearing through the trees.

As he ran, Curt cursed himself. Once again because of him, his friends were at the mercy of the Brotherhood. They had gladly taken the risk, but that didn't change the fact that he had gotten them into the mess. It was up to him now to get them out of it.

The moment he and Mars topped the ridge and got a look at the monastery in panorama, Jaeger knew that it was going to be no easy job.

"I'd say their status is 'full alert,' wouldn't you?" Mars said.

"Yeah, at least," Jaeger replied. The entire compound was armed and either taking up defensive positions near the buildings or working guard patrols with the dogs. There was also a command car running up and down the dirt roads inside the fenced area.

"We're never going to get in there in daylight," Mars said.

"We can't wait," was Curt's answer. "We've got to move. And we've got to do it now."

"You aren't kidding, are you?"

"No, I'm not kidding."

Mars looked at the monastery, then smiled. "Well, I'll say one thing. Going in there at high noon is the last thing they'll ever expect."

Chapter Ten

Goga Tepes led the way through the monastery. Every once in awhile he would glance back over his shoulder at Sondra and Jonas, and smile. As he did so, the skin of his face tightened over the lumps of scar tissue in his cheeks and chin, making them stand out in high relief.

Neither of his two captives said anything. And there wasn't room for them to do anything. On either side they were flanked by men armed with submachine guns. Ahead, between them and the giant Rumanian, walked the old man Curoscu and Tepes's shadow, Ante Palac. They allowed themselves to be led through a doorway and into a whitewashed, windowless room. It was a recent addition to the place. A remodel job. The floor was smooth concrete and it sloped to the center, where there was a large drain covered with a grate. In the ceiling was a fan and exhaust vent.

None of that bothered Jonas Arnstein. What bothered him was the table set to one side—a stainless-steel operating table, and above it a high-intensity surgical lamp. There were machines against the wall on the other side of the table, squat dark machines with round dials and heavy electrical cords running to the wall.

"What do you think of my guest room?" Tepes asked Jonas.

Ante Palac giggled and nodded.

"They used the same interior decorator at Buchenwald," Jonas replied.

"Ah, well, so you aren't surprised. But your girlfriend here, how about her?"

Sondra eyed the Rumanian with contempt. "If it's supposed to intimidate me, it doesn't. There's nothing you can do to make me answer your questions."

"Questions? I have no questions."

Sondra looked at Jonas.

"I know that you were accompanied to the ridge by two men," Tepes said. "They cannot escape. My men will find them and bring them back, dead or alive. You see, there is nothing for you to keep secret. I don't care who you are or where you're from or who sent you. You're going to die, both of you. At my whim."

"Like the two newsmen?" Jonas said.

Tepes shook his head. "No, not like them. There will be nothing public about your deaths. I had them dumped in a ditch to give a warning to snoopers to stay away. A second such warning would only cause trouble, bring attention to the monastery. No, you will die and then disappear like all the others. I command extensive grounds

136

here. There are any number of places where bodies can be hidden permanently."

"Someday you'll be made to pay for all you've done," Jonas said .

Tepes laughed. So did Palac and Curoscu.

"Pay?" Tepes said. "Do you know how many of your people I've killed? Well, neither do I. During the war I shot Jews until my shoulder was black and blue, until it bled. Then I aimed my rifle at others and made them do my shooting for me. That was more than thirty-five years ago. Thirty-five years without punishment. No one is going to make me pay, Arnstein. No one cares."

Jonas stared at the operating table.

"The only question, I suppose," Tepes went on, striding around the room, "is exactly how you two will die." He stopped in front of Sondra. "You're quite attractive for a member of your race," he said. "Perhaps I should arrange a little diversion for my men with you? Say strap you naked to the table and let all twenty of them use you until you die?"

The black-haired girl glared at him.

"Ha! Curoscu, what do you think of that idea?" Tepes said to his old mentor. "You'd be the only one left out of the fun. The only one without steel in his sabre."

Curoscu grinned, showing the stumps of his teeth. "I enjoy other things," he said, leering at Sondra and fingering the handle of his dagger.

"Do you think he's cute?" Tepes asked

her. "A lot of women do. The woods around here are full of them."

Ante Palac shivered with mirth, clutching his round belly with both hands. The other men in green laughed, too.

Sondra just stood there, watching them with cold eyes. As she did, she stretched out the fingers of her right hand, then curled them closed, squeezing tighter and tighter until they made a fist, until her knuckles were white from the strain. She waited, her whole body relaxed except for the fist.

When Tepes turned toward her, she struck with all her might, aiming the blow directly under his sternum, a blow calculated to stop his heart.

The Rumanian staggered back a step, a puzzled look on his face, as if he were unsure of what had just happened. Then he smiled. "Was that the best you can do?" he said.

Sondra cradled her right hand in her left. It felt like she'd hit a concrete wall. She didn't answer his question. She snap-kicked at his head.

Tepes easily dodged the blow by leaning back. The guards closed in on her, grabbing her arms, holding them pinned to her sides.

"I think you should lay down, my dear," Tepes said, gingerly rubbing his sternum. "Over there."

Sondra fought in vain. She was dragged to the operating table and strapped down.

"You bastard!" she cried. "You dirty stinking bastard!"

Tepes walked over to the table, opened a cabinet door set in the side of it, and took something out which he then palmed. He leaned over Sondra and pushed his other hand up under the front of her sweater, exploring.

"No!" she cried, trying frantically to twist away from his touch.

Tepes jammed his free hand down over her mouth, wedging a hard rubber ball between her teeth. He held it in place while he wrapped surgical tape around the back of her head, over the ball and back around, many times. When he let go of her head, it made a solid thunk on the table top.

"See?" he said to Jonas. "See how easy it is to make a woman shut up?"

"Whatever you're going to do to her, do it to me instead," Arnstein told him. "Do it to me and let her go. I beg of you."

Tepes looked around at his men. "Do it to you?" he said. "I hardly think that would be as much fun." He put a proprietary hand on her right breast, squeezing it roughly.

Suddenly there was a commotion at the room's entrance. A man in a business suit was pushing the green shirts, trying to barge in.

"Let me in, goddammit!" Welch said.

Tepes moved closer to the doorway. "No, keep him out," he said. "This is a private matter." He frowned at the men in green

139

gathered around the table. "All right, the rest of you, all except Curoscu and Palac, out, too!"

The men in green filed out and shut the door behind them.

"Well, this is cosier, isn't it?" Tepes said. "Are you comfortable, my dear? Too many clothes on, perhaps? Help her with her clothes, Curoscu."

The old Rumanian whipped out his dagger and set about cutting the clothes from her body. Palac helped him rip them away.

"No, stop!" Jonas said, throwing himself at them, shoving them aside. "Keep back!"

"Was that force you used, Arnstein?" Tepes said. "The great pacifist using force to get his way?"

"Stay back!" the old man warned. He fumbled in a drawer under the operating table and found a surgical knife which he brandished.

"Pacifism goes out the window, huh?" Tepes said.

"I haven't hurt anyone, yet," Jonas said. "I would never hurt anyone else in defense of my own life, but in the defense of another. . . ."

"Like I said, out the window," Tepes told him. He dropped his hand slowly to his holster, unsnapped the flap and drew out the long pistol. "Put down the knife or I'll blow her brains out."

Jonas winced as the Rumanian cocked and aimed the gun at Sondra's face.

"Put down the knife."

Jonas let it drop and started to move back.

"No, old man, you have a part in this, too," Tepes said. He looked down at Sondra, at her nakedness, and smiled. "Can you guess what his part is?" he said to her.

Even if she could have guessed, there was no way she could have made it audible. Tepes grabbed Jonas by the shoulder and pulled him up close to the table. Then he put the muzzle of the gun into Arnstein's ear.

"If you don't cooperate," Tepes said to Sondra. "I'll put a bullet through his head."

"Don't!" Jonas said. His eyes were full of tears. "Not because of me! He's going to kill me anyway."

"Yes, that's true," Tepes said. "But if you don't do as I say, I will do it right now, in front of you. It will be on your conscience alone."

Sondra did not move. She stared up at the ceiling. Whatever thoughts were in her mind at that moment were her own.

When Tepes put a hand on the inside of her knee and pushed her legs apart, she did not struggle. She was like clay, like a dummy, like the dead.

"I'm second," Curoscu said, jockeying for position behind Tepes.

"No, me next!" Palac protested, grabbing the older man by the neck and throwing him back.

141

"Shut up, both of you!" Tepes snarled. He was glaring down at Sondra. "I can see we're going to have a further problem here. The Jewess thinks she's going to sleep through the whole thing. Isn't that right?"

Sondra closed her eyes.

"You think we're going to be satisfied having sex with a zombie? Sorry, but that just won't do. We like a little movement, some response, don't we?"

Palac and Curoscu nodded.

"I'll tell you what we're going to do," Tepes said. "We're going to give you a little incentive to humor us in this. Something guaranteed to make you change your mind in a hurry. Curoscu, open one of her veins. Let's see the color of her blood."

"No!" Jonas said, reaching out to stop the old Rumanian.

The two ancients struggled for a moment, then Ante Palac broke up the match. He hit Jonas in the stomach, doubling him up, then shoved him across the room.

Curoscu drew out his dagger and grabbed Sondra's hand, turning the inside of her wrist up.

"Wait," Tepes said, putting a hand on the old man's shoulder. "Maybe she's changed her mind already. Well, girl, are you going to cooperate?"

Sondra shook her head from side to side.

Tepes let go of Curoscu's shoulder. The old man slashed Sondra's exposed wrist with his knife. She groaned briefly as the blade bit into her flesh, then was silent.

Bright red blood gushed from the wound onto the stainless-steel table.

"When you get in the mood," Tepes said, "just nod your head and we'll stop the bleeding."

Sondra turned her face to the wall and closed her eyes.

The three Rumanians stood around the operating table, waiting for a sign of submission that never came.

Chapter Eleven

Jonas Arnstein offered no resistance when Tepes and the others pushed him into the wooden armchair. He felt the straps being applied to his wrists and ankles, but they did not matter. He had relearned a lesson he'd been taught in the death camps. No matter how many times one witnessed the murder of friends, the pain was always the same.

The operating table had been rolled over closer to the drain in the floor, so that the fluid that sloshed on its surface could flow away. The pretty woman on the table was beyond what happened to her blood. She was beyond everything.

Arnstein flinched when something cold was pressed to the back of his arm. He could not see what it was, but it stayed there when Palac drew his hand away, and from it trailed an electrical cord.

"Did they have machines like this at Buchenwald?" Tepes asked. He was standing over by one of the squat cabinets. He touched some buttons on the machine's front panel, and it began to hum.

Jonas could feel the vibrations through the soles of his feet. "There is nothing you can do to me that you haven't already done," he said.

"I think you're wrong, there," Tepes said. He lightly touched a red button.

The shock hit Arnstein's arm. It was like being kicked by a bull. His arm jerked violently, the muscles contracting, the horrible numbing ache building and building until a ragged cry burst from the old man's lips.

Tepes shut off the current.

"Make him twitch!" Palac said. "Make him twitch again!"

Tepes gestured for Palac to be patient. "I think we need more electrodes," he said.

Jonas felt his shirt being torn open, then the front of his trousers. Cold discs touched his nipples, his penis, his testicles. He told himself that he didn't care what they did to him, that it didn't matter, that he was ready to die, that he had seen enough of human frailty, perversity to last him a hundred lifetimes. He told himself he didn't care, but when Tepes touched the red button again, he knew it was a lie.

The current made his whole body go rigid and the numbing, muscle busting ache filled him from chest to balls. It made him scream. He smelled burning flesh, his own, and screamed even louder.

Tepes shut off the current. A series of sounds outside the door had distracted him. There was some sort of ruckus going on. "See what's happening, Palac," Tepes said impatiently.

The plump man walked to the door and opened it, only to be hurled aside by the man in the business suit.

"Oh, Christ!" Dick Welch said as he took in nude body on the operating table, the old man strapped to the armchair.

Four men in green surged into the room after Welch, and he fought them off with straight, hard punches. Punches that he wasn't pulling. The men in green were taking the worst of it.

"Enough!" Tepes said, waving the troopers back. "Get out. Leave us."

Welch looked again at the table, then glared at Tepes.

"You wanted so much to see, Mr. Welch," the Rumanian said. "Go ahead, examine to your heart's content. Perhaps you'd like to pull the switch on this old Jew?"

"You're a sick son of a bitch, Tepes," Welch said. "Somebody should've yanked your ticket a long time ago."

"Come now. You know how to use this equipment. You probably have used it, right? Hypocrisy doesn't become you."

"I've never used that junk," Welch said. "That stuff is for dementos, senile dementos like you, and third-world highway patrols."

"That is the Central Intelligence Agency talking, Arnstein. What do you think of that?"

Jonas opened his mouth. His lips formed the word "Help," but no sound came forth.

"Arnstein?" Welch said, looking at the man in the chair more carefully. "Arnstein the Nazi hunter?"

"He'd take a bow but he's strapped in."

"He uncovered your identity and you're going to kill him for it?"

"You sound concerned. You shouldn't be. This has nothing to do with you. He's not even a U.S. citizen. I am. You should be concerned about me, not him."

"I am concerned about you or I wouldn't be here," Welch said. He looked over at Curoscu and Palac, sizing them up, measuring their threats to him. They were negligible. He reached into his shirt pocket and took out his pen. Absentmindedly he began tapping his chin with it. "Killing this man could have serious repercussions."

"How so?"

"He's famous. If he disappears around here people will come looking. That could open a whole can of worms." Welch moved closer to Tepes.

"Frankly I don't see any problem. He doesn't have to disappear here. We can dump his corpse five hundred miles away."

"With electrode burns all over it?"

Tepes eyed Welch strangely as the man approached him. His hand dropped to the butt of his pistol. Welch stopped advancing. "Perhaps your company would like to handle the disposal for me?" Tepes said.

"My company would prefer that there was nothing to dispose of, that you let Arnstein go."

"It's a little late for that, I'm afraid," Tepes said, gesturing at the operating table. "This Jew isn't the kind to keep his mouth shut."

Welch put the pen back into his shirt pocket. He had encountered a problem not covered on the instruction sheet. That is, the suspicion caused when one suddenly produces a pen for no apparent reason, when there are no papers to be signed, no documents to go over. He was determined to go through with the killing, though it meant he had to use his gun, and using his gun would bring the whole monastery down on him. Every time he looked at the girl on the table, it made his stomach churn. He wanted to haul his piece out now and empty all fourteen shots into Tepes's face, but he knew his chances of succeeding were slim. Tepes could easily outdraw him because his holster was at his hip instead of behind his back. What Welch needed was a momentary diversion.

"That's quite a nice pen," Curoscu said.

Suddenly Welch knew where he was going to get his diversion. "Yeah, it's okay."

"Can I see it?"

Welch frowned at him. Then shrugged. "Sure, why not," he said. He took the pen from his pocket and unscrewed the cap. Curoscu was standing to one side, away from Palac. Welch stepped between the old Rumanian and his comrades, blocking their view of the proceedings.

"Very nice," Curoscu said as the CIA

man held the pen up in front of his nose. Curoscu reached up to grab it. His fingers never touched it.

Welch shot the poison right in the old man's face. Curoscu jerked his head back, but it was too late. He'd already inhaled. Almost instantly his face turned very dark red. He clutched at his throat and dropped, hitting the floor in a jerking, spasmodic heap.

"Oh, Christ!" Welch said. "I think the old bastard is having a goddam coronary!"

"Curoscu!" Tepes cried, rushing forward, pushing Welch out of the way. He knelt down beside his old comrade and scooped the limp, frail form up into his arms. "Curoscu! Don't leave us!"

Welch knew that the Old Rumanian was long gone. He backed up, slipping his hand inside his suit jacket.

"Get some help!" Tepes shouted at Palac. "Get a doctor! Don't just stand there!"

Palac stopped grinning and scurried for the door.

Welch did not want the door opened. He did not want help from the green shirts. Curoscu was beyond the services of a doctor. He drew his Smith and Wesson out, and as Palac hurried past he cracked him across the side of the head with the muzzle. Palac dropped like a stone.

Tepes saw the gun in Welch's hand and stopped keening over his lost mentor. "What's the gun for? Why did you hurt Palac?"

"Like I said before, it's high time someone yanked your ticket, Tepes." Welch aimed the gun at the big Rumanian's chest.

"You can't! You must not!" Tepes told him. "I have important work to do. It is unfinished."

"Your important work never started," Welch said. "That's why the company gave me the green light to terminate you at my own discretion. You've turned into something of an embarrassment to the agency."

"No, listen," Tepes said. "All this time I've been secretly organizing men in the old country. They are almost ready to strike. We can bring down the regime. We can return democracy to Rumania."

"Bullshit. The only men you've got are right here. And you and your Iron Guard assholes never had anything to do with democracy. Your forte was beating Jews to death and stealing their property."

"If you want me to beg, I will beg," Tepes said.

"Isn't that what you have been doing? How does it feel when the shoe's on the other foot?"

Tepes's eyes glanced away from Welch's face, to the floor beside him. It was a fleeting movement, but Welch caught it. Too late. Palac sank his teeth into the CIA man's leg, savaging it like dog.

Even as the pain hit him, Welch knew he'd blown it. He fired the Smith and Wesson. The slug hit a body, all right. A dead body. Tepes was holding up his old friend as a shield. Welch fired again and again, desperately .

Then the big .44 Magnum boomed deafeningly in the closed room. Welch did not experience the impact of the bullet at the point of its entry. He felt it from the top of his head to his feet. It lifted him off the ground and hurled him against the legs of the operating table. His entire right side was numb. The Smith and Wesson was still in his hand but he could not operate his fingers. He could see the torrent of blood flowing from the great hole in his shoulder but he could feel nothing.

Palac ripped the pistol from his hand, then kicked the operating table away from the drain.

Welch slipped to his back. His head hit the concrete. He was laying in a sea of blood. His blood. Stranger's blood. Goga Tepes loomed over him, the huge gun in his hand.

"You killed Curoscu, didn't you?" Tepes said. "You murdered him?"

Welch smiled. It was starting to hurt. He was feeling the tip of the iceberg. The iceberg was going to be a real bitch.

"How?" Tepes said. "How did you do it?"

"Company secret," Welch said.

Tepes aimed the .44 Magnum at his left thigh and pulled the trigger. Again the room rebounded with the gun's roar.

Welch's leg jerked as if flicked by a giant finger. And when it stopped jerking, it didn't work anymore. Neither did his toes.

"I can take you apart, piece by piece," Tepes said.

"I'm not going to beg," Welch said, through clenched teeth. "I'm not a hunk of slime like you."

"You'll beg, all right," Tepes snarled. The Magnum boomed again and again. And Welch's body jerked up from the floor from the horrendous impact of those heavy slugs.

"Beg! Beg!" Tepes cried, the hammer of his pistol falling over and over on empty cylinders. Then he stopped pulling the trigger.

The CIA man was smiling. He wasn't breathing. But he was smiling. He hadn't begged. He would never beg.

Tepes kicked the corpse in the head. "Palac!" he said, opening the cylinder of his revolver and dumping the spent casings on the floor.

The rotund Rumanian appeared front and center. Except for a fresh crease across the side of his hairless pate he was none the worse for wear.

"Drag this garbage into the corner," Tepes told him.

Palac took the CIA man by the heels and hauled him across the cement floor. As he did, he left behind a wide swathe of red.

Tepes reloaded his pistol, then slipped it back into his holster. He walked over to Jonas and smacked him across the face. "Wake up, old Jew," he said. "Rest period is over."

"I wasn't resting."

"I know. Too noisy. I have a surprise for you. Do you know the current that I used on you before? The current that hurt so much it made you scream?"

Jonas said nothing.

"Well, answer me! Do you know what I'm talking about?!"

"Yes, I know."

"That's better. Well now that horrible, painful current that I used wasn't even a tenth of the power that beautiful little machine can generate. Not even a tenth! Can you imagine what's in store for you next?"

Jonas looked him straight in the eye. "Yes, I think I can."

Chapter Twelve

Once again Jaeger and Mars descended the slope from the rock ridge. They trotted downhill, through the thickets of trees, picking winding paths around the densest of the obstacles. When they reached the bottom, they came up against the twenty-foot-high electrified fence.

Curt pointed to the left, in the direction away from Mars's cabin, the direction of the woodlot. They ran in silence for more than a mile, then Jaeger signaled a stop.

"What is it?" Mars said. He seemed slightly winded from the exertion.

"This isn't getting us anywhere," Curt said. "There's no way to get over the top of the fence. They've got the trees all cut back on this side."

"And we didn't bring anything to jump the voltage with," Mars said.

Curt picked up a twig and flicked it at the wire. Suddenly the dead metal came to life. It hissed, crackled, and a bright blue arc burst around the bit of wood, which in turn burst into flame.

"God knows how many volts they've got

running through that thing," the sandy-haired man said. "I think we'd be taking our lives in our hands trying to jump and cut that wire."

"What alternatives have we got?"

"Remember the gate back the other way?"

"The one Jonas and the girl were taken through?"

"That's right. I think that's the only way we're going to break the security on this place."

"Go in through the goddam gate, huh? And how are we going to pull this off?"

"With your great acting ability. Come on, I'll explain when we get to the gate."

Jaeger turned and started running back the way they'd come. Mars followed close behind. As they approached the gate, the sandy-haired man took a higher route on the side of the hill, keeping out of sight of anyone patroling close to the fence perimeter. He stopped upslope from the padlocked gate and knelt down.

"Okay, now what?" Mars said as he joined him.

"Now we're going to wait until we see a lone green shirt walking near the gate, then we're going to walk down there and yell at him to let us in."

"Just like that?"

"You're going to be leaning on my shoulder and hopping on one foot like you hurt your leg. I'm going to be telling the guy to hurry up because you probably broke something in a fall on the ridge. When he opens up, we take him out."

"Where do you come up with these things? If this guy decides to shoot first, we aren't going to stand a chance."

"Yeah, but I don't think he'd risk shooting a couple of his buddies without making sure. And if we keep our heads down until he's real close. . . ."

"Okay, okay, we'll do it."

Jaeger smiled at him. He knew it was shaky, but it was the best shot they had. They had a lot of ground to cover in a short time. They had to be bold or they'd blow it.

When the lone man in green approached, Jaeger gave Mars a nudge. The legionnaire was about twenty-five yards from the fence. He was walking with his HK at the ready. Curt and Mars hurried down the hill, Mars leaning on Curt's shoulder and hopping on one foot. Curt held their weapons in his free hand.

"Hey!" Jaeger called as they came up to the gate. "Hey, over here!"

The guard looked at them, and as he did, he swung his submachine around, bringing it to bear on them.

"Come on, this guy's hurt!" Curt said. "He fell up on the ridge. Open the gate. Let us through. Hurry!"

The green shirt took a few steps closer, then stopped. He didn't recognize them.

"I think he's broken his leg, dammit,"

Jaeger said. "Are you going to help or not?"

The guard seemed to put aside his caution. He started walking toward the gate. "I'm not supposed to open the gate," he said. "We're on full alert. You know that."

"Yeah, and I know if it was you with a busted leg, you'd want to get back to the monastery in a straight line instead of hopping all the way around."

"Settle down," the green shirt said, reaching into his pocket for his keys.

As he came up to the fence, Curt turned to Mars, angling his face away and blocking the man's view of Mars.

"You didn't see anybody while you were up there, did you?" the guard said as he inserted a key in the electric switch box, cutting the power to the fence. "No, nobody," Curt said.

"Hurry, please," Mars said.

"Yeah, yeah," the legionnaire said, unlocking the padlock and pushing the gate open. "Here, let me give you a hand with him."

Jaeger and Mars jumped the astonished man, driving him back against the fence. There was no time for Marquis of Queensberry rules. Both Mars and Jaeger swung on the guy. Mars hit him on the chin and Curt hit him in the belly. He went limp in their hands.

"Strip the belt off him," Mars said. "We can tie him up with it."

They quickly cinched the legionnaire's

hands behind his back and then tied his wrists to his ankles. They gagged him with his own handkerchief and left him behind a bush twenty feet up the hill. Then they gathered up their weapons and walked through the open gate.

"Just like clockwork," Curt said, closing the gate behind him. He closed the padlock and turned the current back on. "Now, let's head for the woods."

They paralleled the fence, walking very close to the dog run, walking as far away from the other men in green as they could.

When they were within fifty yards of the edge of the woods, the command car appeared to the right off in the distance, traveling at an easy pace down the dirt road that divided the cleared area from the grove of trees.

"Jesus, look!" Mars said. "They're coming our way."

"Yeah, I can see," Curt said. "Keep moving."

Jaeger picked up the pace a little. Not enough to draw attention to themselves. One of the men in the command car stood up and pointed at them. The driver of the car sped up almost at once, leaving a trail of dust in his wake.

"They're onto us!" Curt said. "Run for the woods! If they cut us off before we get there, we're dead meat."

Mars needed no encouragement. He broke into a full out sprint, and Curt was hard pressed to keep up. They crossed the dirt

163

road just as the command car was closing in on them. Someone in the car shouted for them to stop. No shots were fired, though. That was a good sign. The men in green still weren't sure they were dealing with a pair of intruders.

Jaeger and Mars pushed deeper and deeper into the dense woodlot. Over the swish of branches against their clothing they could hear the command car screeching to a halt on the road.

"Cut right," Curt said.

They turned and went another fifty yards before stopping. Jaeger looked at Mars's face. It was dripping with sweat. "How many did you see in the car?" Curt said.

"Five, maybe six."

"We're going to have to take them out in here," Jaeger told him. He stripped out of his pack and put down the M16. There wasn't room to manuever the automatic rifle. The trees were too thick.

"Bare-handed?" Mars said.

"You object?"

"No. No, I don't object." The red-haired man dumped his weapon, too. "I guess we should split up."

"Right. You stay here and I'll move closer to the road. Don't move after you hear my footsteps stop. The only way we're going to be able to tell where these guys are is by sound."

"Got ya."

Curt moved away, working around a particularly dense patch of trees, then traveling in a more or less straight line until he was within twenty-five yards of the road. He found a small depression at the base of a large dead tree and squatted down in it. It felt strange not being armed and going up against men with automatic weapons, but Jaeger knew that the advantage was his in the heavy cover. A man with a gun would try to use it before he did anything else. By the time an opponent got his muzzle up between a gap in the tree trunks, Curt would be on top of him. Or at least that was the idea.

Jaeger waited, listening. In a matter of minutes he heard sounds coming from the road. It was as he'd suspected. The legionnaires were fanning out along the dirt track before penetrating the forest. That way they could keep their quarry from slipping around or through them.

The crunch of shoes on dry leaves grew louder and louder. Jaeger took a peek from around his cover. A lone greenshirt was approaching. He could see no others, but he could hear them, moving in a rough line into the woods.

He waited until the man had passed, roughly within fifteen feet of him, then he attacked. He sidestepped his way through a gap between two trees and dove at the man's legs.

The green shirt cried out as he was hit and knocked face down in the leaves. Curt jammed his face deeper into the pile of leaves, muffling his cries. The man's weapon was pinned under him, useless. Jaeger rode the thrashing, kicking body for a minute or two, then took the man by the shoulder, abruptly rolled him face-up and socked him on the chin. He hit him three times and the third time he felt the nose give way under his fist. There wasn't time to tie the man up, so Curt just tossed his weapon into another pile of leaves and moved on.

He was aware at once of someone calling to his left. The name that was being shouted wasn't his. "Yo!" he said in answer to the shout.

"Are you all right?" was the reply.

Jaeger zeroed in on the direction of the shout. Up ahead, in the maze of tree trunks, the confusing crisscrossing of shadow and light, he saw movement. He circled carefully and once again came up behind his enemy.

"Where are you?" the man in green shouted in the wrong direction.

Curt charged. Only this time, his opponent managed to react to the sound, managed to turn and raise his submachine gun. Jaeger cut to the left, dodging between tree trunks. The green shirt tried to track him with his muzzle. The muzzle came to a sudden stop against a branch. The stop was so startling to the legionnaire that he touched the trigger, setting off a brisk burst.

Before he could raise the gun and free it from the branch, Curt was on top of him.

Jaeger held the HK aside and down and hit the man with a chopping right hand across the windpipe. The legionnaire gasped and gurgled. Curt hit him in the solar plexus and he went down.

Again Jaeger tossed the weapon into the bushes and moved on. Deeper in the grove he heard the sounds of struggle, then a withering burst of automatic weapon fire. He hoped that Mars had handled it. If he had, there was only one more green shirt left. If he had been handled, instead, there were two.

Jaeger plunged into the woods, moving back to where he'd left Mars. Something moved up ahead, and he stopped. The something was holding a submachine gun. A sinking feeling hit him in the pit of his stomach. Maybe Mars hadn't made it after all

He advanced on the lone figure, coming up on his blind side in a sudden mad rush. The figure turned, dropping to a crouch, swinging the HK through an unobstructed arc that ended on a line with Jaeger's chest. There was no hail of lead, however.

"How did you do?" Mars said, lowering the weapon.

Jaeger looked at the pair of bodies laying face-down in the leaves. "About as well as you," he said. "I thought we were going to do this bare-handed?"

"Yeah, well, the one on the left didn't want to let go of his HK and by the time I convinced him, I had his buddy there to deal with, so I hammered them both. I hammered quite a few trees, too."

"I can see that. Let's get our gear and get a move on."

When they'd picked up their weapons and Curt had donned the pack, he pointed in the direction that they'd come. "We're going that way," he said.

"That's the wrong way," Mars said. "The monastery's over there."

"Yeah, I know, but the command car's over there. We stand a better chance riding to the target than walking, don't you think?"

"Right."

They hurried through the woods, stopping at the edge and looking out at the parked convertible command car. The driver was sitting on the top of the front seat, looking over the windshield, his submachine gun ready to rip.

"How are we going to do this one?" Mars said. "Another straight-on run?"

"Why not?" Curt said.

They stepped out of the trees and started walking casually toward the car. The driver let them come about ten paces before he opened fire.

"Damn!" Curt said, diving away from the string of slugs. He rolled and came up firing.

Mars rolled in the opposite direction and also came up shooting. The front windshield of the car disintegrated in the crossfire. And the driver was knocked ass-over-teacup into the rear seat.

Jaeger was the first to reach the car. The driver's legs were sticking up in the air. They weren't moving. They weren't ever going to move again.

"Let's get him out," Curt said.

They dumped the corpse on the ground and jumped into the car. Curt started up the engine, threw the car into gear, and roared off down the road.

"Get those RAWs hooked up to the M16s," he told Mars. "We're going to need them quick."

The red-haired man opened the pack and took out the HE projectiles and their launching brackets. In a matter of seconds he had them connected to the barrels of the automatic rifles.

They raced past a two-man dog patrol. The green shirts turned to stare. Mars waved at them. "How close are you going to try and get?" he said.

"Close enough so we can avoid any obstacles to our getting into the building." He followed the road around and headed toward the main compound. No one seemed to be paying special notice to them. When they were within seventy-five yards of the monastery, Curt stopped the car.

"This is close enough," he said, reaching for one of the M16s. He held up the weapon and removed the safety pin from the RAW's bracket. Then he jacked a live round into the rifle's chamber and propped the stock on the top of the shattered windshield. He aimed the black-and-white rocket at the side of the building.

"What are we aiming for?" Mars said.

"I say we make ourselves a new doorway," Curt told him. "How about there, between those two windows on the left."

Mars pulled his safety pin, cocked his weapon and propped it on the windshield, too. "Got ya," he said. "On the count of three?"

Jaeger counted down, and when he said "Three!" they both fired. The standard military hard-ball rounds activated the rocket's firing sequence. As the bullets left the muzzles, some of the emergent gas was directed down a hole in the brackets, against the RAW firing pins, which in turn hit percussion caps that started the rocket motors.

As the projectiles launched, the muzzles of both rifles lifted from the sudden loss of weight and the launch tubes under the barrels spun madly.

There was a flash of hard light at the side of the building, then an explosion as the two spherical projectiles flattened against the target, then detonated. Smoke and debris fountained into the air and a large ragged hole appeared in the formerly solid wall.

Even before the debris settled, Curt and Mars were out of the car and running for the new doorway. Jaeger hit it first, his M16 out in front of him. The hole was more than ample, even for a man of his size. He stepped into a smoke-filled room. Before the blast it had been occupied by a pair of green shirts. They now lay against the far wall, which was splattered with their blood and brains.

Curt waited for Mars to clear the hole, then opened the door to the hall, peering out and seeing men in green running all over the place. "It's a madhouse already," Jaeger said. "Let's take advantage of it while we can."

The two men darted out into the hall and headed for the center of the building. There were legionnaires all over the place, but none seemed to be paying any attention. Curt and Mars walked among them with impunity.

"What do you think?" Mars said as they rounded a turn and came upon the dining hall.

"I think we'd better find out where Tepes is," Curt said.

The next legionnaire who came running past met a solid obstacle. Jaeger's right hand. The man crashed to the floor. Curt grabbed him by the collar and dragged him to the side.

The guardist's eyes opened wide when he realized that he was looking into the face of his enemy. "You aren't . . . hey! Hey!" he started to shout.

Curt jammed the muzzle of the M16 into the man's open mouth, ramming it past the edge of his teeth. The shouts stopped

171

at once. "What we want to know is," Curt said, "where did Tepes take the old man and the girl?"

The legionnaire's face contorted. It was clear that he was fighting some kind of inner battle. Should he tell or should he die like a good soldier, taking the secret to the grave with him?

Curt pushed more M16 into his face.

The inner battle was over as quickly as it had begun. The green shirt nodded frantically. Curt pulled the muzzle back.

"They're on the other side of the dining hall," the guardist said. "Around the next turn, the only door on the left side."

"Thanks," Curt said, leaning down and cracking the man across the jaw with his clenched fist. The man's head snapped to the side and stayed there; his eyelids fluttered shut.

"Oh, Jesus!" Mars said suddenly.

Curt looked up just in time to see a half dozen armed legionnaires come running down the hall. They didn't ignore Jaeger and Mars. They started shooting.

Both men ducked back behind the dining room entrance just as the hail of hot lead sailed past. Jaeger was on one side of the gap and Mars on the other. Across the gap was no man's land.

"Damn!" Curt said, hitting the wall with his fist. It was no time to get pinned down. Not only were his friends still in mortal danger, but the longer he and Mars waited the more likely it was that reinforcements would attack them from the other side of the dining hall.

"Ready?" he shouted to Mars.

Mars just looked at him.

"Ready to take those guys out?"

"You're kidding."

Bullets whined down the hall, through the entrance, passing between them like angry bees.

"We've got no choice. It's either go for it now or wait until we get caught in a crossfire from behind."

Mars shook his head. "Why is it with you there's never a choice?"

"I say we both go at the same time, both go low, belly down and we mop up on them."

"Yeah, well, we might as well."

"On the count of three again?"

Mars nodded. He counted down this time. At the same instant both he and Curt threw themselves out into the fire lane, diving belly down on the floor, their automatic rifles up hard against their shoulders.

There wasn't time to think. There was only time to act. Hot slugs sailed all around them, skipping off the floor in front of their faces, cutting chips out of the wall above their heads.

Curt lined up on a green shirt caught flat-footed in the middle of the hall. One squeeze took the man out. Curt rode the recoil, using it to swing the sights onto his next target.

Chapter Thirteen

Something cold hit Jonas Arnstein in the face. It startled him and brought him out of his faint. He blinked the water from his eyes and looked up at his torturer.

"We're up to half power, now," Tepes said. "It's a bit different than when we began, isn't it?"

"Very different," Arnstein said from between clenched teeth. He did not look down at himself, at the damage the electrodes had already done to his body. He did not want to see it. He could smell it, smell the aroma of his own burnt flesh, and that was more than enough. He kept telling himself that he was an old man, that the next shock would be enough to kill him, to set him free from the agonizing torture, but so far his physiognomy had proved much more substantial than he'd guessed.

"How much should I give him this time, Palac?"

"All of it! Fry him!" the rotund green shirt said.

Tepes shook his head. "No, we must save

177

that until the very end. We must stretch out the pain. That's how we play this little game."

Tepes adjusted the voltage regulator and jabbed the red button with his thumb. At once the room lights dimmed from the amount of electricity drawn through Jonas's body. Jonas did not see that, though. He saw only white, blinding white, as the current flashed through his head. It made his body do things against his will. It made him crash his teeth together. It made him go utterly rigid. It made him wet his pants. And for as long as Tepes held the button in, as long as the current raged through him, he was held in a limbo of pain.

When Tepes let up on the button, the old man slumped back in the armchair, his head lolling on his shoulders, his mouth open.

"More water," the Rumanian said. "The way he keeps passing out is beginning to irritate me."

Palac passed him a pail of water which he dumped on top of Arnstein's bald head.

"Ohhhh," Jonas moaned, jerking awake, gasping for breath.

"You disappoint me," Tepes told him. "We are just halfway up the scale and you can't seem to stay awake. I'm going to have to do something about that."

Palac grinned as he watched his lord and master advance the voltage regulator by another quarter.

"We'll try some short bursts now, and see how you like them."

Jonas took a breath and held it, shutting his eyes, tensing his muscles against the pain that he knew was about to come. There was no way to prepare himself for it, though. When Tepes touched the button, his body tried to jump up from the chair, hurling itself against the bonds, his head snapping back again and again against the back of the chair. Then it stopped.

For a moment Jonas was too stunned to do anything. His heart was beating wildly, irregularly, in his chest. Then a low moan escaped his lips.

"See, you didn't pass out," Tepes said. "That's much better."

Jonas felt his spirit retreating to the furthest corner of his mind. He had come very close to dying that time. His heart had almost stopped. The next time. Or the time after that. He would be released. He was ready to go.

"He doesn't look so good," Palac said. "His face is so gray."

Tepes laughed. "You wouldn't look so good either if you'd just had a couple of hundred volts put through your penis."

"No, I mean, he looks like he's going to die."

Tepes leaned down and peered at Arnstein's face examining his eyes. "Are you going to die on me so soon, old man?" he said. "You're not going to spoil my fun,

179

are you? We've only just begun. There's a full quarter of the dial to explore. Where is your sense of adventure? Your pioneering spirit?"

Jonas could not speak. There was nothing he wanted to say anyway. He knew that anything he said would only serve to give the monster pleasure, and pleasure was the only thing he could withhold now. He could die in silence and dignity. He closed his eyes and prayed. He prayed that the next flash of light would be the last thing he ever saw.

"I'm going to turn the voltage up a bit more," Tepes told him. "Just a hair. We can't have you getting used to it. That would ruin the effect."

Jonas did not try and steel himself. He knew that it was useless to fight such an overwhelming force. His mouth was parched and his head was spinning. He could not keep his fingers from trembling against the arms of the chair.

"Stand clear," Tepes said. Then he hit the button again.

Arnstein hadn't thought anything could have been worse than the last time, but this was. The contractions of his muscles were so strong that it felt as if his spine would snap under the strain. His body arched, throwing itself against the bonds. He could not breathe, could not see, could not think about anything but the pain, the burning, numbing pain.

Then the whole building was rocked by

a terrible explosion. Plaster fell from the ceiling and walls, bottles tumbled from open cabinets and smashed on the floor.

"What was that?!" Tepes cried, taking his hand from the controls. "God, what was that?!"

Palac just stood there looking stunned.

"Something blew up," Tepes shouted at him. "Go on, hurry, see what it was." He pointed at the door.

Palac reluctantly left the room.

Jonas slowly came around. As he regained full consciousness, he groaned. He was still alive. Alive to face yet another blast of raw power.

"Something blew up," Tepes repeated for Arnstein's benefit.

The old man wasn't in the least bit interested.

"Probably one of those young idiots accidentally set off a hand grenade. But that doesn't mean we have to interrupt our little session." Tepes put his finger to the red button again.

Jonas moistened his lips. This had to be the one. It just had to.

Tepes jammed the button down. Nothing happened. He pressed it again. And again nothing happened.

Jonas looked at him with a puzzled expression.

Then they both heard the hard popping sounds of rifle fire down the hall.

Chapter Fourteen

Curt fired again, the M16 bucked against his shoulder, and a second green shirt dashing desperately for an open doorway in the hall never reached it. He went down in a thrashing, kicking heap. And suddenly there were no more targets and the fusillade from the opposition ceased. Those who had been able had ducked out of the hall; those who hadn't lay sprawled on the floor.

Jaeger looked over at Mars. The red-haired man was holding aim along the line of the wall. When an HK muzzle poked out of a doorway, he cut loose with a three round burst. The muzzle disappeared.

"What now?" Mars said.

Curt grimaced. They had turned the tables on the legionnaires and taken control of the hallway, but there was no way to press their advantage. They couldn't advance without walking into a wall of hot lead. They couldn't do a room-to-room search-and-destroy to eliminate the threat of the surviving green shirts.

"We've got to go," he said, gesturing

over his shoulder with his thumb. "Let's do it now while they're still thinking."

The two of them retreated at a run, crossing the dining room and entering the hall on the other side. They paused just inside the entrance, and when a legionnaire poked his head out of the hallway on the other side of the room, Curt and Mars both cut loose with their rifles. They didn't hit him, but they made him duck back so quickly that he dropped his weapon.

As they turned away, facing down the new hall, Curt saw a door click shut on the right. He pointed at it, then advanced to it. Mars moved to the other side of the hall, rifle at his shoulder, ready to back up the play on the other side of the door, or to stop anyone from entering the hall.

Curt reared back and kicked the door with his foot, breaking it free at the lock. It swung inward, exposing a rotund little man cowering amid the mops and brooms and buckets.

"Out," Jaeger said.

Ante Palac got to his feet and slinked out into the hall. He shot a furtive glance down toward the dining room.

"Don't even think it," Mars said, aiming the M16 at his stomach.

"I want to know about Tepes," Curt said. "Is he alone?"

Palac nodded energetically.

"Armed?"

Again Palac nodded.

"Then you're going to get us in to see him."

Palac stopped nodding. Curt grabbed him by the collar and shoved him ahead. Mars walked backwards, keeping an eye on the hall behind. They rounded the turn in the hall without seeing another green shirt. When they came to the lone door on the left, Curt pulled Palac up close.

"You're going to knock on that door," Jaeger told him. "Announce who you are. Then say that your guys killed the intruders. Then you're going to open the door and all of us are going in. Do you underand?"

Palac understood, but he was not pleased. He had begun to perspire profusely.

"Go ahead and knock."

The plump Rumanian stepped up to the door and raised his doughy hand. He paused, took a breath, swallowed, then rapped on the wood twice.

Curt gestured with his rifle.

"It's Palac," the legionnaire said. "We got them, Goga. We killed them both."

As he reached for the door knob, Mars and Curt swung in behind him. They let him turn it and start to open it, then pushed him against and through the doorway.

Almost at once there was a deafening boom. And the little plump man turned into a rag doll—a rag doll flung back between them and out the doorway.

Curt already had his weapon shouldered

as the door swung clear. He saw the tall man with the hogleg pistol. He fired a second after Tepes. So did Mars.

The twin 5.56mm slugs caught Tepes in both shoulders at once. The impact didn't knock him down, but it drove him back four steps. And it made him drop his gun.

"Stay right there," Mars said, holding his sights steady on the man's lumpy face.

Curt kicked the door shut and shot home the locking bolt. It was only when he turned back that he saw Sondra on the stainless steel table. For an instant, blinded by fury, there was only one thought in his mind. He swung the sights of his rifle onto Tepes's chest. He would have pulled the trigger, but a sound, a moan from the other side of the room made him pause and seek out its source.

"God, Jonas!" he said, lowering the M16 and hurrying over to the armchair.

Arnstein looked at him for a second without understanding. Then he said, "I thought I was dead. No, I hoped I was dead."

Curt gently undid the restraints from his wrists and ankles. "Can you walk?"

Arnstein tried, but his knees were too weak.

"That's all right, I'll carry you."

"There's no place for you to carry him too," Tepes said. His grin was frozen on his face. A grin of pain. Blood flowed freely down both his arms and dripped onto the cement floor. "There's no way out of this room but that way." He pointed at the door. "And my men will be waiting for you. You won't get ten feet."

"That's what we're counting on," Curt said. "That all your men will be outside the door because they know there's no other way out."

Tepes gave him a puzzled look. He was not particularly concerned about the danger he was in. He believed that his life could be traded for a safe exit for his captors.

Jaeger unshouldered his pack and took from it another RAW and firing bracket. He discarded the one he'd already used and replaced it with the new one.

"You're not going to shoot that thing off in here?" Tepes said. "You'll kill us all."

"Everybody back," Curt ordered.

Mars waved Tepes to the side with his gun, then helped Jonas to safety.

Jaeger fired the rocket from a distance of thirty feet. Because the spherical head of the projectile flattened on impact, it essentially provided a shaped charge. Though most of the force of the explosion was outward, the concussion of the blast in the closed room was awesome.

When the smoke cleared, there was a large hole in the wall.

"Okay, let's go," Curt said to Tepes, who was still staring in shock at the new doorway. There would be no trade for safety. "If you want me to shoot you again, I will, but you're coming with us."

Mars went through the hole first, then helped Jonas through. Curt guarded the rear as Tepes squeezed past the opening, then followed. He didn't look back at what lay on the table. He didn't have to. He could see it far too clearly in his mind's eye. It was a vision of horror that would be forever in his memory.

There were no green shirts waiting for them on the outside. Curt picked up Arnstein and started trotting back for the command car. Mars drove Tepes ahead of him with the muzzle of his M16.

When they reached the car, Curt put Jonas in the back seat and Mars climbed in with him. "Get in the front," Curt said to Tepes.

As the Rumanian sat down in the passenger seat, Mars put the muzzle of his M16 to the back of his head. "Sneeze and your brains are going to be a hood ornament," Mars told him.

Curt removed his pack and put it in the back seat, then got behind the wheel and started the car. "You'd better rig up with another RAW," he told Mars. "We're going to need it to create a way out of here."

"This can't be happening," Tepes moaned. "My men, where are my iron men?"

At that moment shots rang out, and ricocheting bullets whined off the dirt, the sides of the car and the side of the monastery. Curt raised up and shouldered his M16, sending an entire thirty-round clip in the direction the shots had come from.

"Let's go," Mars said, fumbling in the back with the RAW bracket.

Curt sat down, threw the car in gear and sped away from the monastery. More bullets sailed around them, and then they were really moving, doing seventy on the dirt road.

"Where should I go?" Curt shouted over the roar of the engine.

"Straight ahead," Mars said. "I know a nice quiet spot that'll be just perfect for an intimate get-together."

Curt bore down on the high electric fence. He ran straight for it. The few legionnaires out and about in the field stood flat-footed, awestruck at the apparent insanity of the driver of the convertible.

"Okay," Curt said. "Let her rip."

Mars got up on the top of the back seat and aimed the rocket at the fence they were rapidly closing upon. He aimed about four feet up from the ground, holding as steady as he could given the wild, bouncing ride. Then he touched off the HE projectile.

It zoomed ahead of the speeding car and hit the fence higher than Mars had anticipated. Not that it mattered. Upon impact, there was a tremendous explosion and arc of electric light.

By then it was too late for the car to have stopped even if they had wanted it to. They roared into the clouds of smoke and shot through a gap that would have accomodated a Mack truck and trailer.

"Keep right," Mars shouted as they rumbled over the turf.

Jaeger fought to keep the car from slipping into a sideways skid when they hit the dirt road. Once he had the car under control, he floored the accelerator again and they roared off down the narrow track.

"There's a turn-off about five miles up," Mars said.

"There's nothing up there," Tepes said shrilly. "Nothing but the old mine."

"That's right," Mars said. "The old mine. Can you think of any place more private?"

Tepes said nothing. He looked straight ahead.

When Curt was within a half mile of the turn-off, he slowed down so as not to miss it. Even then, Mars had to point it out to him. There was no sign, only a rutted dirt road cutting back at an angle from the track they were on. He had to make a K-turn to manage it. Then they were bouncing along under a canopy of birch trees. The road wound back and forth and finally ended in a large clearing.

The clearing abutted the steep side of a hill. In the middle of the open space was a three-story building made of corrugated metal. It was dark with rust. From the top story of the building to the ground was a dilapidated conveyor belt housed in a frame of girders. Alongside the building was a pool of stagnant water.

Curt parked the car and turned back to Mars. "Well?" he said.

"The mine entrance is over there," Mars answered, pointing with his rifle. "On the other side of the building."

Curt stared at Arnstein for a long moment. "Are you going to be all right, Jonas? Do you need a doctor?"

The old man shook his head. "I'll be okay."

"Are you sure?"

"Yes, positive."

The two men locked gazes. Curt knew that Jonas was aware of what was going to happen inside the mine. By asking the old man if he wanted a doctor, he had offered to delay or even put off forever what he had in mind for Goga Tepes. He had done this out of respect for Arnstein and for what Arnstein and Sondra had suffered at Tepes's hands. But the old man, knowing what was being offered, had refused—in effect, giving his blessing to Jaeger.

It was a blessing Curt accepted with reluctance. Arnstein's outspoken pacifism had been a great help to him. It was a standard by which his own actions in the name of justice could be measured. Looking at the old man's haggard face, he could not help but wonder if all the humanitarianism had finally, inexorably, been beaten from him.

"All right," he said to Tepes, "get out of the car."

"You can't just kill me," the Rumanian said.

Curt reached over the back seat and took

his custom-made single-shot handgun from the pack. He cracked open the bolt and inserted a live round in the chamber. "Get out of the car," he repeated, locking down the bolt and pointing the gun at Tepes's temple.

The tall Rumanian slowly opened the door and backed out. Curt got out the driver side and rounded the front of the car. "Toward the mine," he said, gesturing with the gun.

"No, please," Tepes said. "You have no reason to kill me. You're not a Jew. You have no vendetta against the Iron Guard."

"If you don't move this second," Curt told him, "I'll drop you where you stand."

The Rumanian stiffened. He considered himself a good judge of character. As such he knew the sandy-haired man wasn't bluffing. He started to walk for the edge of the rusty mine building. He walked right through the stagnant pond, not seeing it, not feeling it. He was already envisioning what was to come in the darkness of the mine.

Chapter Fifteen

It was cool in the mine shaft. The moment they stepped into the shadows at its entrance, the air temperature dropped a good fifteen degrees.

"That's far enough," Curt said. "Sit down on the ground."

Tepes obeyed, moaning as he had to put pressure on his wounded shoulders to lower himself. "Who are you?" he said. "What do you want?"

There was a sniveling edge to the man's voice that turned Curt's stomach. "My name is Jaeger," he said. "I'm the son of a man you undoubtedly have heard of. Horst von Jäger."

"Von Jäger! But he's a Kameradenwerk. Like me. If you're his son, then you're one of us. Why are you doing this to me?"

"I may be like you, but I'm not one of you," Jaeger said.

"I don't understand."

"No more questions," Curt told him. "Just answers. Do you know where my father is?"

Tepes made no reply.

197

"Is he in Paraguay?"

The Rumanian shrugged.

"I want an answer, dammit!"

"If I tell you what you want to know will you let me go?"

"I'm not going to make any deals with you," Curt told him. "As far as I'm concerned, you're already dead. The only thing in doubt is the manner of your passing and the extent of your pain. It's a game I'm sure you've played many times before."

"But you could let me go. No one would know. You could just walk away."

"You played the game with Sondra, didn't you?" Curt said. He leaned forward and jabbed the muzzle of his gun into the wound in Tepes' right shoulder.

"Ahhh!" Tepes cried, shrinking back.

"That little poke was nothing," Curt said. "You know it was nothing. You know how far the game can go. Is my father in Paraguay?"

"Yes, as far as I know."

"Where?"

"He doesn't stay in the same place all the time," Tepes said. "He's part of the leadership, the inner circle, and they all move around together. They take turns staying at each other's ranchos."

"Sounds unlikely."

"No, it's true. They do it so they can keep an eye on each other. So they can make sure no one of them is trying to overthrow the others."

"Which rancho is my father staying at now?"

"There's no way of telling, not from here. The inner circle doesn't announce its moves. They all just pack up and go."

Curt considered this for a moment, then said, "Are all of these ranchos close by?"

"Yes, they all share common borders. The enclave is in the middle of the Chaco Boreal."

"They also share protection?"

"In part."

"Your guardsmen?"

"My guardsmen protect the inner circle."

"What about the local police and military?"

"They stay away. The Kameradenwerk doesn't need them. It makes its own justice in the Chaco. It has an army of native soldiers who patrol the outskirts of its territory and make sure that no one trespasses and lives to tell about it."

"How many troops do they have?"

"A few thousand. And if they aren't enough, the inner circle has been known to call in a few regular Paraguayan Army units to help out for special occasions."

"The government doesn't object?"

"The government pretends not to notice. You see, ODESSA commands a state within a state. It has its own borders. It sets its own policies. And its enterprises out earn those of the larger state a thousand times over."

"How does ODESSA keep tabs on all that?"

"Satellites. It has its own telecommunications system. Everything can be run from the safety of the Chaco. The members of the inner circle rarely leave the enclave. And even more rarely set foot outside Paraguay."

"Understandable considering that they all have been sentenced to death in absentia for war crimes."

"What can you possibly gain from any of this?" Tepes said.

"I intend to go to Paraguay."

"You'll die there."

"Maybe. But not before I kill Horst von Jäger."

"You'll never even get close to him. It's different in South America. Much different than here. You'll be dead before you learn the rules."

"I make my own rules," Jaeger said. "That's how I'm like you. There's a world of difference between our goals, though."

"Really?"

"You, my father and the rest of the Kameraden are after wealth, power at any cost. All I want is to destory you and yours. So far I've succeeded. If your Iron Guard was supposed to be the best the Brotherhood has to offer, they didn't stand up too well, did they? I walked right into your stronghold and kicked the hell out of them, kidnapped you out from under their noses."

Tepes was silent for a moment. Then he said, "You'll live to regret what you've done today. My legionnaires will hunt you down. Be sure of it."

"You're dreaming," Curt said. "They'll bury their dead and then go back to their crops and livestock. The evil dies with you, Tepes. It dies here, today, right now. Stand up!"

"No, God, not like this!"

"Why should it be any different for you than for your victims? Stand up, it's time."

When the Rumanian refused to move, Jaeger put the muzzle of his pistol to the man's forehead and said, "Get up or you'll die where you sit."

Tepes staggered to his feet, sobbing, pleading.

"I wish your Iron Guardsmen could see you now," Curt said.

"God, oh, God," Tepes muttered.

"Turn and face the tunnel," Curt told him.

The Rumanian stood still.

"Turn away from the light," Jaeger repeated, bringing the barrel of his gun down hard on the man's shattered shoulder.

Tepes moaned and stumbled, almost falling on his face. Then, slowly, on legs of lead, he turned and looked down the mine tunnel into the smothering blackness.

"No more light," Curt said, raising the muzzle of the handgun to the back of Tepes's head. "Not for you. Only darkness. Darkness and the pit."

As he squeezed down on the trigger, Curt opened his mouth wide and yelled as loud as he could to counteract the terrible force of the concussion blast in the enclosed space. Still, the roar of the pistol shot in the mine shaft was horrendous. It shook loose a rain of rock fragments from the ceiling; it rattled the timbers and walls.

Curt Jaeger turned away from the corpse and stepped quickly out into the sunlight. Behind him, the sound of the single gunshot echoed over and over. A chorus of dissonant bells, ringing the death knell for Goga Tepes.

He walked around the shallow puddle and got into the Mercedes. Neither Mars nor Jonas said anything to him. There was nothing to say. Mars started up the car and turned it around, heading it back down the tree-lined dirt road.

Curt stared straight ahead, blind to the rutted track, the stands of birch, the blue sky. All he could see was the end. The end of his war against his father and the Brotherhood.

The end was Paraguay.